THE SETTING SUN

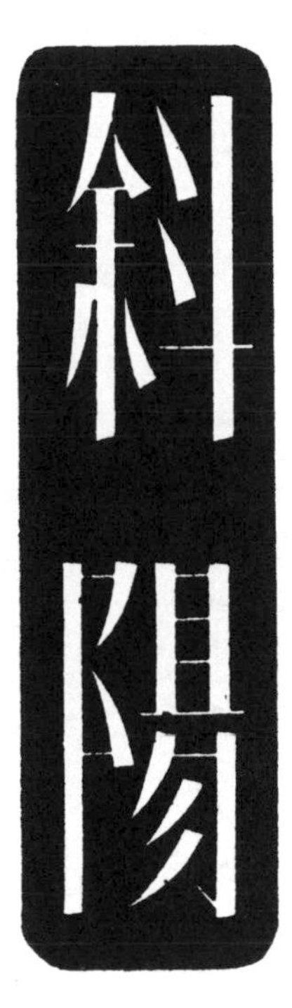

THE SETTING SUN

BY OSAMU DAZAI

TRANSLATED BY DONALD KEENE

A NEW DIRECTIONS BOOK

Library of Congress Catalog Card Number: 56-13350.
ISBN-13: 978-0-8112-0032-5.

Manufactured in the United States of America. First published as New Directions Paperbook 258 in 1968.
New Directions Books are published for James Laughlin by New Directions Publishing Corporation, 80 Eighth Avenue, New York 10011

39 38 37 36 35 34

CONTENTS

Note on Pronunciation of Names

Japanese in transcription is pronounced with the consonants as in English and the vowels as in Italian. Thus, the name Naoji is pronounced nah-oh-jee. There is no marked stress accent, and one is safe in giving equal weight to all syllables.

In this novel most of the characters (such as Naoji, Kazuko, and Osaki) are referred to by their personal names only. Where both personal and family names are given, the family name comes first. Thus, in the name Uehara Jirō, Uehara is the family name and Jirō the personal name.

Translator's Introduction

The foreign visitor to Japan today is apt to be at once delighted and dismayed by what he observes. The delight will probably stem from what is old in the country—the temples set in their clean-swept grounds and gardens, the brilliant spectacle of the theatres, the cordiality and charm of one's reception in any Japanese home. Most travelers indeed are so captivated by this aspect of Japan as to become excessively critical of what the past sixty or seventy years have brought from the West. They bewail the fact that many Japanese women have given up their beautiful kimonos in favor of mass-produced dresses, that the Japanese house is all too frequently marred by a "foreign-style" room with lumpish furniture obscurely derived from European prototypes, and that the streets are filled with the din of clanging trams and squawking loud-speakers. Those who complain in these terms are quite justified in their aesthetic indignation, although not in the arrogant impatience with which it is too often accompanied.

Japan today, alone of the nations of Asia, is closely connected to the West, not only in its industrial and political developments, but in its active cultural life. The bookshops are full of European (especially French) works of literature in translation, including all the latest and most difficult ones. There are numerous coffee-shops where students gather to listen to records of Beethoven and Brahms, if not of Debussy and Stravinsky. Even the banks send out calendars all over the country with excellent reproductions of Renoir, Van Gogh, or Matisse. It may be debated how deeply this interest in modern Western literature and art penetrates, whether the farmer in his village has any better understanding of Goethe or Manet than his grandfather did. The fact remains that almost everywhere in Japan education has brought with it a profound respect for Western culture, and sometimes a genuine love.

This feeling has often been indiscriminate and led to a defacement of the Japanese landscape which we may find all but unpardonable, but it has not been only adulation for the West which has led to many of the changes so deplored by the foreign visitor. The Japanese woman who abandons the traditional kimono in favor of a dress is not merely imitating some Hollywood star; she is liberating herself from the nuisance of the elaborate series of robes and underrobes, unbearably hot in summer and impractical at any time of the year in the offices and busses she must cope with today. Even if she would like nothing better than to wear a kimono every day, the cost of the expensive silks makes the traditional costume a luxury which few can afford unless they have inherited them.

The face of Japan is changing every day as taste, convenience, and economic necessity dictate. Underneath the surface, at an undeniably slower pace, the moral and spiritual life of the country is undergoing similar change. The family system is breaking up, especially in the larger cities, and the traditional values associated with the family are losing ground. Divorce, for example, is now accepted (at least in Tokyo) as the alternative a woman has to an odious marriage, although until very recently she was expected to accept the flagrant infidelity of her husband and any other indignity he might choose to inflict on her in the interest of preserving the family. It will take years for such new ideas to spread throughout the country, but even today few of the younger people share their parents' belief in the traditional views.

As far as religion goes, one would have to look very hard to find in Japan even as much fervor as exists in this country, let alone India. Although most Japanese are nominally Buddhists and are buried, for form's sake, in accordance with Buddhist ritual, real interest in the religion is comparatively unusual. If, for example, the Prime Minister of Japan were to adopt the practice of important political figures in the United States and England (and elsewhere, of course) of invoking the blessings of the Deity—any deity—on the heads of the Japanese people, he would be greeted with astonishment and possibly derision. It may seem strange that Japan, which has borrowed so much from the West, has never taken more to Christianity. There has in fact been a decline of interest in Christianity since its high point at the turn of the century when many of the intellectual leaders were devout believers in a "churchless" Protestantism. This form of Christianity has not proved satisfying to most of their descendants who, even if they remember the Bible lessons of their childhood, find in them no adequate solution to their present problems.

The people whose lives are described in *The Setting Sun* are in many ways exceptional, but they are also typical of modern Japan. Kazuko, the girl who relates the story, seems more accustomed to wearing Western clothes than kimonos, is reminded as often of Chekhov or Balzac as of *The Tale of Genji*, and, if not fluent in any Western language, uses a variety of French and English phrases with certainty that she will be understood by everyone. At the same time, she remains unmistakably Japanese in her relations with the people around her and in her quick emotional responses to the moments of intensity in her life. Because family confidences are almost impossible (except on the rare occasions when the repressions of Japanese life are overcome by the force of intolerable emotions), Kazuko, her mother, and her brother live almost without overt communication with one another. The author, Dazai Osamu, must therefore resort to various types of flashback techniques (including a diary, letters, and a will) to create for us three-dimensional figures. And although he succeeded in lending extraordinary vividness to his characters, there is much necessarily left unsaid in this Japanese world. *The Setting Sun* owes much to European culture, but it is as Japanese a novel as can be written today, in this period when the surface and inner manifestations of Japanese life are being Westernized at very different speeds and when (to a Western reader) the Japanese literature which reflects these changes is surprising, alternately, for its closeness and remoteness to our own lives.

"Victims of a transitional period in morality" is how Kazuko styles herself and her lover, and we feel that she is right. A *modus vivendi* with Western *things* has nearly been achieved, but the full effect of Western ideas has yet to be felt. *The Setting Sun* derives much of its power from its portrayal of the ways in which the new ideas have destroyed the Japanese aristocracy. The novel created an immediate sensation when it first appeared in 1947. The phrase "people of the setting sun," which came to be applied, as a result of the novel, to the whole of the declining aristocracy, has now passed into common usage and even into dictionaries. Kazuko, her mother, and her brother Naoji are typical not only of the aristocracy but of the large class of Japanese who were impoverished by the war and the succeeding inflation and land reforms.

In reading the novel one cannot escape the feeling that the author, Dazai Osamu, himself was personally involved—that he was not only the story-teller but a participant. An examination of his biography tends to confirm this impression. Dazai was born in 1909 of a rich and powerful family of the north of Japan. He was brilliant in his studies at school and early showed promise of his literary talent, as well as signs of the erratic habits which were subsequently to darken his career. Before he was twenty, he twice attempted suicide. In 1930 he entered the Department of French Literature at Tokyo University. Dazai knew no French when he elected this course (and apparently, through complete neglect of his studies, never learned more than a few words), but at the time French literature was the chosen field of many young Japanese. This was partially because they found French Symbolism or Surrealism more congenial than the more matter-of-fact English literature, and far more so than the philological problems of the classical Japanese literature, and partially because of the universal credence given in Japan to legends surrounding the magical *vie de Bohème* of Paris.

Dazai withdrew from the University in 1935 without obtaining a degree. This was not surprising when one considers that he boasted of not having attended a single lecture in five years. Instead, he spent his time in literary and Left-Wing political activity. His stories had begun to attract attention when in 1935 he again attempted suicide, leaving in an envelope a collection of fourteen of his stories with the title, *Declining Years,* which was intended for posthumous publication. Dazai had, in the meantime, become addicted to morphine and was forced to spend almost two years in and out of hospitals before he could be cured. In 1936 there was another suicide attempt, this time with the woman with whom he had been living for the previous six years. He was married in the following year to another woman, who still survives him today.

Dazai's life of wild dissipation gave him much notoriety and caused even some unpopularity. This was especially true during the austere years which preceded the war with the United States. He was exempted from military service because of a chronic chest ailment. During the war he continued to publish, although he was forced by the bombings to move from one part of the country to another.

His most important literary activity came after the end of the war. Early in 1947 he published his brilliant short story "Villon's Wife" (which has been included in *New Directions 15*) and, later in the same year, *The Setting Sun,* the present volume. His second novel, *The Disqualified,* appeared in 1948 and was acclaimed by some critics as being even superior to *The Setting Sun.* He also began the serial publication of another novel with the English title of *Good-bye.* The cumulative effects of dissipation, overwork, and insomnia gave him an appearance of such utter exhaustion as to alarm his friends. The tuberculosis from which he had suffered before the war and which he claimed to have cured by drinking again manifested itself. The symptoms were unmistakable. In June of 1948 he finally succeeded in committing suicide, by throwing himself into the swollen waters of the Tamagawa Reservoir in Tokyo. Ironically enough, his body was discovered on his thirty-ninth birthday, the nineteenth of June.

The close connection between Dazai's life and almost any of his works is immediately apparent, although as an artist he naturally did not confine himself to a mere recounting of autobiographical details. *The Setting Sun* is actually one of his more objective works, and yet we may find much in Naoji, in the novelist Uehara, his mentor, and even in the girl, Kazuko, who narrates most of the story, that clearly derives from Dazai's own personality and experiences. Dazai, himself a member of a near-aristocratic family, chose to depict the decline of his own class. Again and again we find ourselves wondering to what degree Dazai shared the emotions of his characters. When

Naoji expresses the pain it has cost him to stay alive, we seem to hear the voice of the author who considered suicide so often. However, what gives *The Setting Sun* a strength that most of Dazai's other writings, however brilliant, generally lack is the character of Kazuko, who is determined to struggle rather than to die. Dazai himself, after his brief and not very animated participation in the Left-Wing movement, seemed to lose all desire to struggle, and his writings are almost invariably tinged with cynical despair.

Dazai's indebtedness to European literature is obvious, but he is in fact more closely linked with the great classics of Japanese literature, with which he was intimately familiar. His style offers no particular problems for the Western reader, but he uses one literary device which, although not unknown in the West, is perhaps unusual. He sometimes gives the last or climactic remark in a conversation first and then goes back to relate the steps leading up to it. An effective device in his hands, it is part of his fondness for the flashback. Another feature of Dazai's style which the reader will note is how he uses the description of minor happenings (such as, the burning of the snake eggs or the swelling in the mother's hand) to suggest much larger situations. In this technique he betrays his debt to Japanese poetry, particularly the miniature, seventeen-syllable haiku, in which each word must be a vital part of the whole, and where the attempt of the author is to make the reader supply from these scant drops the world from which the poem has been distilled.

It is generally conceded that Dazai is one of the great chroniclers of contemporary Japanese life, and this major achievement was reached despite the shortness of his life and career. He creates for us with amazing evocativeness a great variety of places—an old-fashioned mansion in the city, a country house, a Tokyo hovel, a cheap bar—and fills them with the people and the atmosphere that belong to them. I am, in a way, tempted to urge the Western reader to turn to Dazai for an exact picture of what life is like in Japan today, although certainly there are other pictures of Japan which can and have been painted of this same period. Despite the specialized area of the subject matter and the deviant behavior of some of its characters, *The Setting Sun*, by the depth of its understanding of the Japanese of today, evokes and reveals aspects of the Japanese nation as a whole. This is why the novel was so successful and so moving to Japanese of all classes. But *The Setting Sun* is not to be considered as a sociological document of help to those who wish to learn more about an obscure or distant country. It is a powerful and beautiful novel by one of the most brilliant of recent Japanese writers and stands as such in the world of literature.

Cambridge-New York Donald Keene

THE SETTING SUN

This translation is dedicated to Kawabata Yasunari, the distinguished novelist and President of the Japanese P.E.N. Club, who has done so much to promote the understanding of Japanese literature abroad.

蛇

CHAPTER ONE / SNAKE

Mother uttered a faint cry. She was eating soup in the dining-room.

I thought perhaps something disagreeable had got into the soup. "A hair?" I asked.

"No." Mother poured another spoonful of soup into her mouth as if nothing had happened. This accomplished, she turned her head to one side, directed her gaze at the cherry tree in full bloom outside the kitchen window and, her head still averted, fluttered another spoonful of soup between her lips. Mother eats in a way so unlike the manner prescribed in women's magazines that it is no mere figure of speech in her case to use the word "flutter."

Naoji, my younger brother, once said to me when

he had been drinking, "Just because a person has a title doesn't make him an aristocrat. Some people are great aristocrats who have no other title than the one that nature has bestowed on them, and others like us, who have nothing but titles, are closer to being pariahs than aristocrats. Iwashima, for example (mentioning one of his school friends, a count), doesn't he strike you as being more vulgar than any pimp you might meet in the streets? That damned fool wore a tuxedo to his cousin's wedding. Even supposing there was some necessity for him to appear in that outfit, it made me want to puke just to hear the highfalutin language the idiot saw fit to use when making a table-speech. That kind of affectation is a cheap front which has nothing whatsoever to do with refinement. Just the way there used to be signs around the University saying 'High-Class Lodgings,' most of what passes for the aristocracy might actually better be called 'High-Class Beggars.' The real aristocrats don't put on silly airs like that Iwashima. Mama is the only one in our family. She's the genuine article. There's something about her none of us can match."

Take the matter of eating soup. We are trained to lean slightly over the plate, to take up a little soup with the spoon held sideways, and then to bring it to our mouth, still holding the spoon sideways. Mother, on the other hand, lightly rests the fingers of her left hand on the edge of the table and sits perfectly erect, with her head held high and scarcely so much as a glance at the plate. She darts the spoon into the soup and like a swallow—so gracefully and cleanly one can really use the simile—brings the spoon to her mouth at a right angle, and pours the soup between her lips from the point. Then, with innocent glances around her, she flutters the spoon exactly like a little wing, never spilling a drop of soup or making the least sound of sipping or clinking the plate. This may not be the way of eating soup that etiquette dictates, but to me it is most appealing and somehow really genuine. As a matter of fact, it is amazing how much better soup tastes when you eat it as Mother does, sitting serenely erect, than when you look down into it. But being, in Naoji's words, a high-class beggar and unable to eat with Mother's effortless ease, I bend over the plate in the gloomy fashion prescribed by proper etiquette.

Mother's way of eating, not only soup but everything else, is quite a thing apart from normal table manners. When the meat appears she at once cuts it up into little pieces with her knife and fork, then transfers the fork to her right hand and happily skewers one piece after another. Again, while we are struggling to free the meat from a chicken bone without rattling the plate, Mother unconcernedly picks up the bone in her fingers and chews the meat off. Even such uncivilized actions seem not only charming but strangely erotic when Mother performs them. The real things are apt to be deviant.

I have sometimes myself thought things would taste better if we ate with our fingers, but I refrain from doing so, for fear that if a high-class beggar like myself imitates Mother badly, it might make me look a beggar plain and simple.

My brother Naoji says that we are no match for Mother, and I have at times felt something akin to despair at the difficulty of imitating her. Once, in the back garden of our house in Nishikata Street—it was a beautiful moonlight evening in the beginning of autumn—Mother and I were sitting in the summer-house by the edge of the pond admiring the moon, when she got up and went into a nearby clump of flowering shrubs. She called to me from among the white blossoms with a little laugh, "Kazuko, guess what Mother is doing now."

"Picking flowers."

She raised her little voice in a laugh. "Wee-wee!"

I felt there was something truly adorable in her which I could not possibly have imitated.

This has been quite a digression from this morning's soup, but I recently learned from a book I was reading how in the days of the French monarchy the court ladies thought nothing of relieving themselves in the palace gardens or in a corner of the corridors.

Such innocence really charms me, and I wondered if Mother might not be one of the last of that kind of lady.

At any rate, this morning she let out a little cry —ah—as she sipped the soup, and I asked if it were a hair, only to be informed that it was not.

"Perhaps it was too salty."

The soup this morning was green pea, from an American can I got on the ration and made into a kind of potage. I haven't any confidence in my abilities as a cook, though it is one of the few confidences a girl should have, and couldn't help worrying about the soup, even after Mother said that nothing was wrong.

"You made it very well," Mother said in a serious tone. After she had finished the soup, she ate some rice-balls wrapped in seaweed.

I have never liked breakfast and am not hungry before ten o'clock. This morning I managed to get through the soup, but it was an effort to eat anything. I put some rice-balls on a plate and poked at them with my chopsticks, mashing them down. I picked up a piece with my chopsticks, which I held at right angles to my mouth, the way Mother holds a spoon while eating soup, and pushed it into my mouth, as if I were feeding a little bird. While I dawdled over my food, Mother, who had already finished her meal, quietly rose and stood with her back against a wall warmed by the morning sun. She watched me eating for a while in silence.

"Kazuko, you mustn't eat that way. You should try to make breakfast the meal you enjoy most."

"Do you enjoy it, Mother?"

"It doesn't matter about me—I'm not sick anymore."

"But I'm the one who's not sick."

"No, no." Mother, with a sad smile, shook her head.

Five years ago I was laid up with what was called lung trouble, although I was perfectly well aware that I had willed the sickness on myself. Mother's recent illness, on the other hand, had really been nerve-racking and depressing. And yet, Mother's only concern was for me.

"Ah," I murmured.

"What's the matter?" This time it was Mother's turn to ask.

We exchanged glances and experienced something like a moment of absolute understanding. I giggled and Mother's face lighted into a smile.

Whenever I am assailed by some painfully embarrassing thought, that strange faint cry comes from my lips. This time I had suddenly recalled, all too vividly, the events surrounding my divorce six years ago, and before I knew it, my little cry had come out. Why, I wondered, had Mother uttered it too? It couldn't possibly be that she had recalled something embarrassing from her past as I had. No, and yet there was something.

"What was it you remembered just now, Mother?"

"I've forgotten."

"About me?"

"No."

"About Naoji?"

"Yes." Then, checking her words, Mother leaned her head to one side and added, "Perhaps."

My brother Naoji was called up while still at the University and was sent off to some island in the South Pacific. We have had no news of him, and he is still missing, even after the end of the war. Mother has resigned herself to never seeing Naoji again. At least that is what she says, but I have never once "resigned" myself. All I can think, is that we certainly will see him again.

"I thought I had given up all hope, but when I ate your delicious soup I thought of Naoji, and it was too much for me. I wish I had been better to him."

Along about the time that Naoji first entered high school he became fanatically absorbed in literature, and started to lead a life almost like a delinquent, causing Heaven only knows how much grief to Mother. And in spite of his dreadful behavior, Mother thought of Naoji as she ate her soup and uttered that cry. I angrily pushed the food into my mouth and my eyes grew hot.

"He's all right. Naoji's all right. Scoundrels like Naoji simply don't die. The ones who die are always the gentle, sweet, and beautiful people. Naoji wouldn't die even if you clubbed him with a stick."

Mother smiled. "Then I suppose that you'll die an early death." She was teasing me.

"Why should I? I'm bad and ugly both! I'm good for eighty years!"

"Really? In that case, your mother is good for ninety!"

"Yes," I said, a little perplexed. Scoundrels live a long time. The beautiful die young. Mother is beautiful. But I want her to live a long time. I was at a loss what to say. "You are being difficult," I protested. My lower lip began to tremble, and tears brimmed over.

I wonder if I should tell about the snake. One afternoon, four or five days ago, the children of the neighborhood found a dozen or so snake eggs concealed in the stakes of the garden fence. They insisted that they were viper eggs. It occurred to me that if we were to have a dozen vipers crawling about our bamboo thicket we would never be able to go into the garden without taking special precautions. I said to the children, "Let's burn the eggs," and the children followed me, dancing with joy.

I made a pile of leaves and brushwood near the thicket and set it afire, throwing the eggs into the flames one after another. They did not catch fire for the longest time. The children put more leaves and twigs on the flames and made them blaze more vigorously, but the eggs still did not look as if they would ever burn.

The girl from the farmhouse down the road called from the other side of the fence to ask what we were doing.

"We are burning viper eggs. I'm terrified that the vipers might get hatched."

"About how big are the eggs?"

"About the size of a quail's egg and pure white."

"Then they're just ordinary harmless snake's eggs and not viper eggs. Raw eggs don't burn very well, you know."

The girl went off laughing as if it were all very funny.

The fire had been blazing for about half an hour, but the eggs simply would not burn. I had the children retrieve them from the flames and bury them under the plum tree. I gathered together some pebbles to serve as a grave-marker.

"Let's pray, everybody." I knelt down and joined

my hands. The children obediently knelt behind me and joined their hands in prayer. This done I left the children and slowly climbed the stone steps. Mother was standing at the top, in the shade of the wisteria trellis.

"You've done a very cruel thing," she said.

"I thought they might be viper eggs, but they were from an ordinary snake. Anyway, I gave them a regular burial. There's nothing to be upset about." I realized how unfortunate it was that Mother should have seen me.

Mother is by no means superstitious, but she has had a mortal dread of snakes ever since ten years ago, when Father died in our house in Nishikata Street. Just before Father passed away, Mother, seeing what she thought was a thin black cord lying near Father's bed, casually went to pick it up, only to discover that it was a snake. It glided off into the corridor, where it disappeared. Only Mother and my uncle Wada noticed it. They looked at each other but did not say anything, for fear of disturbing the peace of Father's last moments. That is why even Naoji and I (who happened to be in the room) knew nothing about the snake.

But I know for a fact from having seen it that on the evening of my Father's death, there were snakes twisted around all the trees by the garden pond. I am twenty-nine now, which means that when my father died ten years ago I was already nineteen, and no longer a child. Ten years have gone by, but my memories of what happened then are still perfectly fresh, and I am not likely to be mistaken. I was walking by the pond intending to cut flowers for the service. I stopped by a bank of azaleas and suddenly noticed a little snake twined around the tip of an azalea branch. This startled me a little. Then when I went to cut off a bough of kerria roses from the next bush, I saw a snake there too. On the rose of Sharon next to it, on the maple, the broom, the wisteria, the cherry tree—on every bush and tree—there was a snake. This didn't especially frighten me. I only felt somehow that the snakes, like myself, were mourning my father's death and had crawled out from their holes to pay his spirit homage. Later, when I whispered to Mother about the snakes in the garden, she took it calmly, and merely inclined her head a little to the side, as if she were thinking of something. She did not make any comment.

And yet it is true that these two incidents involving snakes made Mother detest them ever after. Or it might be more correct to say that she held them in fear and awe, that she came to dread them.

When Mother discovered that I had burned the snake eggs, she certainly must have felt that there was something ill-omened in the act. This realization brought home to me the feeling that I had done a terrible thing in burning the eggs. I was so tormented by the fear that I might have caused an evil curse to fall on Mother that I could not put the event out of my mind, not that day, or the next, or the next. And yet this morning in the dining-room, I had blurted out that idiotic remark about the beautiful dying young, which I could not cover up afterwards, no matter what I said, and had ended up in tears. Later, when I was clearing up the breakfast dishes, I had the unbearable sensation that some horrible little snake which would shorten Mother's life had crawled into my breast.

That same day I saw a snake in the garden. It was a beautiful, serene morning, and after finishing my work in the kitchen, I thought I would take a wicker chair out onto the lawn and do some knitting. As I stepped down into the garden with the chair in my arms, I saw the snake by the iris stalks. My only reaction was one of mild revulsion. I carried the chair back to the porch, sat down, and began to knit. In the afternoon, when I went into the garden intending to get from our library (which is in a storehouse at the bottom of the garden) a volume of Marie Laurencin's paintings, a snake was crawling slowly, slowly over the lawn. It was the same snake that I had seen in the morning, a delicate, graceful snake. It was peacefully crossing the lawn. It stopped when it reached the shade of a wild rose, lifted its head, and quivered its flame-like tongue. It appeared to be searching for something, but after a few moments dropped its head and fell to the ground, as though overcome with weariness. I said to myself, "It must be a female." Then too the strongest impression I received was one of the beauty of the snake. I went to the storehouse and took out the volume of paintings. On the way back I stole a glance at where I had seen the snake, but it had already vanished.

Toward evening, while I was drinking tea with Mother, I happened to look out at the garden just as the snake again slowly crawled into view, by the third step of the stone staircase.

Mother also noticed it. "Is that the snake?" She rushed over to me with these words and stood cowering beside me, clutching my hands. It flashed into my mind what she was thinking.

"You mean the mother of the eggs?" I came out with the words.

"Yes, yes." Mother's voice was strained.

We held each other's hands and stood in silence, watching the snake with bated breath. The snake, languidly coiled on the stone, began to stir again. With a faltering motion it weakly traversed the step and slithered off toward the irises.

"It has been wandering around the garden ever since this morning," I whispered. Mother sighed and sat heavily on a chair.

"That's what it is, I'm sure. She's looking for her eggs. The poor thing." Mother spoke in a voice of dejection.

I giggled nervously, not knowing what else to do.

The evening sun striking Mother's face made her eyes shine almost blue. Her face, which seemed to wear about it a faint suggestion of anger, was so lovely that I felt like flying to her. It occurred to me then that Mother's face rather resembled that of the unfortunate snake we had just seen, and I had the feeling, for whatever reason, that the ugly snake dwelling in my breast might one day end by devouring this beautiful, grief-stricken mother snake.

I placed my hand on Mother's soft, delicate shoulder and felt a physical agitation which I could not explain.

It was at the beginning of December of the year of Japan's unconditional surrender that we left our house in Nishikata Street in Tokyo and moved to this rather Chinese-style house in Izu. After my father died, it was Uncle Wada—Mother's younger brother and now her only surviving blood relation—who had taken care of our household expenses. But with the end of the war everything changed, and Uncle Wada informed Mother that we couldn't go on as we were, that we had no choice but to sell the house and dismiss all the servants, and that the best thing for us would be to buy a nice little place somewhere in the country where the two of us could live as we pleased. Mother understands less of money matters than a child, and when Uncle Wada described to her our situation, her only reaction apparently was to ask him to do whatever he thought best.

At the end of November a special-delivery letter arrived from my uncle, informing us that Viscount Kawata's villa was for sale. The house stood on high ground with a good view and included about half an acre of cultivated land. The neighborhood, we were told, was famous for its plum blossoms and was warm in winter and cool in summer. Uncle Wada's letter concluded, "I believe that you will enjoy living there. It is apparently necessary, however, for you to have a personal interview with the other party, so would you please come tomorrow to my office?"

"Are you going, Mother?" I asked.

"I must," she said, smiling in an almost unbearably pathetic way. "He asked me to."

Mother left the next day a little after noon. She was accompanied by our former chauffeur, who escorted her back at about eight the same evening.

She came into my room and sat down with her hand against my desk, as if she might collapse on the spot. "It's all decided," were her only words.

"What has been decided?"

"Everything."

"But," I said in surprise, "before you have even seen what kind of house it is?"

Mother raised one elbow to the desk, touched her hand to her forehead, and let out a little sigh. "Uncle Wada says that it's a nice place. I feel as if I would just as soon move there as I am, without even opening my eyes." She lifted her head and smiled faintly. Her face seemed a little thin and very beautiful.

"Yes, that's so," I chimed in, vanquished by the purity of Mother's trust in Uncle Wada.

"Then you shut your eyes, too."

We both laughed, but after our laughter had died away, we felt terribly depressed.

The workmen came every day to our house from then on, and packing for the move began. Uncle Wada also paid us a visit and made the necessary arrangements so that everything which was to be sold could be disposed of. Okimi, the maid, and I were busy with such tasks as putting the clothes in order and burning rubbish in the garden, but Mother gave us not the slightest assistance. She spent every day in her room dilly-dallying over something.

Once I screwed up the courage to ask her, a little sharply, "What's the matter? Don't you feel at all like going to Izu?"

"No," was all she answered, a vague look on her face.

It took about ten days to complete the removal

preparations. One evening when I was out in the garden with Okimi burning some waste-paper and straw, Mother emerged from her room and stood on the porch, silently watching the blazing fire. A cold greyish wind from the west was blowing, and the smoke crawled over the ground. I happened to look up at Mother's face and was startled to see how poor her coloring was, worse than I had ever seen it before.

"Mother, you don't look well!" I cried. Mother answered with a wan smile, "It's nothing." She moved soundlessly back to her room.

That night, because our bedding had already been packed, Okimi slept on a sofa while Mother and I slept together in her room on bedding borrowed from a neighbor.

Mother said in a voice which sounded so old and weak that it frightened me, "I am going to Izu because you are with me, because I have you."

I was taken aback by this unexpected remark. "And what if you didn't have me?" I asked in spite of myself.

Mother suddenly burst into tears. "The best thing for me would be to die. I wish I could die in this house where your father died." She spoke in broken accents, weeping more and more convulsively.

Never had Mother spoken to me in such a feeble voice, and never before had she let me see her weeping with such abandon. Not even when my father died, or when I was married, or when I came back to Mother pregnant, or when the baby was stillborn in the hospital, or when later I was sick and confined to my bed, or, for that matter, when Naoji had done something bad—never had she shown such weakness. During the ten years since Father's death, Mother had been just as easy-going and gentle as while he was alive. Naoji and I had taken advantage of her to grow up without concerning ourselves about anything. Now Mother no longer had any money. She had spent it all on us, on Naoji and myself, without begrudging us a penny, and she was being forced to leave the house where she had passed so many years to enter on a life of misery in a cottage without a single servant. If Mother had been mean and stingy and scolded us, or had been the kind of person who secretly devises ways to increase her fortune, she would never have wished for death that way, no matter how much times had changed. For the first time in my life I realized what a horrible, miserable, salvationless hell it is to be without money. My heart filled with emotion, but I was in such anguish that the tears would not come. I wondered if the feeling I experienced then was what people mean by the well-worn phrase "dignity of human life." I lay there, staring at the ceiling, feeling incapable of the slightest motion, my body stiff as a stone.

The next day, as I had expected, Mother seemed definitely ill. She lingered over one thing and another as if every additional minute she could remain in the house was precious to her, but Uncle Wada came to inform us that we had to leave that day for Izu. Almost all the luggage had already been dispatched. Mother with obvious reluctance put on her coat, and bowing without a word to Okimi and the other people in our employ who had come to say good-bye, she walked out of our house in Nishikata Street.

The train was comparatively empty, and we were all able to find seats. My uncle was in extremely good spirits and hummed passages from the No plays, among other things. Mother, pale and with her eyes downcast, looked very cold. We changed at Nagaoka for a bus, rode for about a quarter of an hour, got off, and began to walk toward the mountains. We climbed a gently sloping rise as far as a little village, just outside which was a Chinese-style villa, built with some taste.

"It's a pleasanter place than I had imagined, Mother," I said, still gasping for breath from the climb.

Mother stood in front of the entrance of the cottage. "Yes it is," she answered, a happy expression coming into her eyes for a moment.

"To begin with, the air is good. Fresh air," declared my uncle with evident self-satisfaction.

"It really is," Mother smiled. "It's delicious. The air here is delicious."

We all three laughed.

Inside we found our belongings arrived from Tokyo. The front of the house was piled high with crates.

"Next, there is a fine view from the sitting-room." My uncle, quite carried away, dragged us there and made us sit down to admire it.

It was about three in the afternoon, and the winter sun was gently striking the garden lawn. At the foot of a flight of stairs that led from the lawn, there was a little pond surrounded by plum trees, and beyond the garden, an orchard of tangerine trees. A village road, rice fields, a grove of pines, and, in the distance, the sea could also be discerned. As I sat in the drawing-room, the sea appeared to be just on a level with my breasts.

"It's a gentle landscape," Mother said dully.

"It must be because of the air. The sunlight here is entirely different from Tokyo sunlight, isn't it? It's as if the rays were strained through silk," I answered with excessive gaiety.

On the ground floor were two fairly good-sized rooms, a Chinese-style reception room, a hall, and a bathroom, then the dining-room and kitchen. Upstairs was a foreign-style room with a big bed. This was the whole house, but I thought that it would not be especially cramped for two of us, or even for three if Naoji returned.

My uncle went out to the only inn in the village to arrange about a meal for us. A lunch was presently delivered which he spread out in the sitting-room and began to eat. Some whisky he had brought served to wash it down. He was very cheerful and insisted on relating his adventures in China with Viscount Kawata, the former owner of the house. Mother barely touched the food, and soon afterwards, when it started to grow dark, she murmured, "I'd like to lie down for a bit."

I extracted the bedding from our baggage and helped Mother spread it. Something about her worried me so much that I ferreted out the thermometer to take her temperature. It was 102 degrees.

Even my uncle seemed upset. At any rate, he went off to the village in search of a doctor. When I called to Mother, she merely nodded drowsily.

I pressed Mother's little hand in mine and began to sob. She was so pitiful, so terribly pitiful—no, we were both pitiful. The tears would not stop. I thought as I wept that I would like to die on the spot with Mother, that we had nothing to hope for any longer, that our lives had ended when we left the house in Nishikata Street.

Some two hours later my uncle returned with the village doctor. He seemed quite an old man and was dressed in formal, rather old-fashioned Japanese costume.

"It may possibly develop into pneumonia. However, even if pneumonia develops, there is no occasion for anxiety." With this rather vague pronouncement, he gave Mother an injection and departed.

Mother's fever did not go down the following day. My uncle handed me 2,000 yen with instructions to telegraph him if it should happen that Mother had to be hospitalized. He returned that day to Tokyo.

I took the necessary minimum of cooking utensils from our baggage and prepared some rice-gruel. Mother swallowed three spoonfuls, then shook her head. A little before noon the doctor appeared again. This time he was in slightly less formal attire, but he still wore his white gloves.

I suggested that it might perhaps be better if Mother went to the hospital. "No," the doctor said, "I do not believe it to be necessary. Today I shall administer a strong injection, and the fever will probably abate." His answer was just as unreassuring as the previous time, and he went away as soon as he had finished giving Mother the "strong injection."

That afternoon Mother's face turned a bright red and she began to perspire profusely. This, perhaps, was to be attributed to the miraculous powers of the injection. Mother said, as I changed her nightgown, "Who knows, he may be a great doctor!"

Her temperature had dropped to normal. I was so happy that I ran to the village inn and bought a dozen eggs from the proprietress. I soft-boiled some at once and served them to Mother. She ate three and about half a bowl of rice-gruel.

The next day the great doctor appeared in his formal costume again. He nodded gravely when I thanked him for the success of the injection, with an expression as much as to say "Exactly as I expected." He examined Mother carefully, then turning to me said, "Your mother has quite recovered. She may therefore eat and do whatever she desires."

His manner of speech was so peculiar that I had all I could do to keep from bursting out laughing. I showed the doctor to the door. When I returned to her room, I found Mother was sitting up in bed.

"He really is a great doctor. I'm not sick any more," she said absent-mindedly, as if she were talking to herself. She had a very happy expression on her face.

"Mother, shall I open the blinds? It's snowing!"

Snowflakes big as petals had softly begun to fall. I threw open the blinds and, sitting next to Mother's side, watched the snow.

"I'm not sick any more," Mother said, once again as if to herself. "When I sit here with you this way, it makes me feel as if everything that has happened was just a dream. To tell the truth, when the time came for moving, I simply hated the thought. I would have given anything to stay a day, even half a day, longer in our house in Nishikata Street. I felt half-dead when I had to board the train, and when we arrived here, after the first moment or two of pleasure, I felt my heart would burst with longing for Tokyo, especially when it grew dark. Then everything seemed to go blank before me. It wasn't an ordinary sickness. God killed me, and only after He had made me into someone entirely different from the person I had been, did he call me back to life."

From that day to the present, we have managed to continue our solitary lives in this cottage in the mountains. We prepare meals, knit on the porch, read in the Chinese room, drink tea—in other words, lead an uneventful existence almost completely isolated from the world. In February the whole village was buried in plum blossoms. One placid, windless day succeeded another well into March, and the blossoms remained on the boughs until the end of the month. At whatever time of the day one saw them, the blossoms were breath-takingly beautiful, and their fragrance flooded into the room whenever I opened the glass doors. Toward the end of March a wind would spring up every evening, and as we sat in the twilighted dining-room drinking tea, petals would blow in through the window into our cups. Now in April our conversation, as we knit on the porch, has generally turned on our plans for cultivating the fields. Mother says she would like to help. Even as I write these words the thought strikes me that, just as she said, we have already died, only to come back to life as different people. But I don't suppose a resurrection like Jesus' is possible for ordinary human beings. Mother spoke as if the past were already forgotten, but all the same, when she tasted the soup this morning she thought of Naoji and uttered that cry. Nor, indeed, have the scars of my past healed.

Oh, I would like to write everything down plainly and absolutely without concealment. I sometimes secretly think that the peace of this house in the mountains is nothing more than a lie and a sham. Even assuming that this has been a short period of respite vouchsafed by God to my mother and myself, I can't escape the feeling that some threatening, dark shadow is already hovering closer to us. Mother pretends to be happy, but she grows thinner by the day. And in my breast a viper lodges which fattens by sacrificing Mother, which fattens however much I try to suppress it. If it is only something which comes with the season, and nothing more! That I could have done such a depraved thing as burn the snake eggs certainly shows what a state I am in. Everything I do seems only to make Mother's unhappiness the more profound and to weaken her.

As for love . . . no, having once written that word I can write nothing more.

火
事

CHAPTER TWO / FIRE

During the ten days that followed the incident with the snake eggs, one ill-fated thing after another occurred to intensify Mother's unhappiness and shorten her life.

I was responsible for starting a fire.

That I should have started a fire. I had never even dreamed that such a dreadful thing would happen to me. I at once endangered the lives of everyone around me and risked suffering the very serious punishment provided by law.

I must have been brought up so very much the "little lady" as not to have been aware of the obvious fact that carelessness leads to conflagrations. Late one night I got up to wash my hands, and as I passed by the screen in the entrance hall, I noticed a light coming from the bathroom. I gave it a casual glance only to discover that the glass door of the bathroom was a glowing red, and I could hear an ominous crackling. I rushed to the side door and ran outside barefoot. I could see then that the pile of firewood which had been stacked beside the furnace was blazing furiously.

I flew to the farmhouse below our garden and beat with all my might on the door. "Mr. Nakai. Fire! Fire! Please get up! There's a fire!"

Mr. Nakai had apparently already retired, but he answered from inside, "I'll come at once." While I was still urging him to hurry, he dashed out of his house, still in his bedclothes.

We raced back to the fire. Just as we began to draw water from the pond with some buckets, I heard Mother call from the gallery next to her room. I threw down my bucket, climbed up to the gallery, and caught Mother in my arms. She was on the point of collapse. "Mother, please don't worry. It's all right. Please go back to bed." I led her back to bed and having persuaded her to lie down, I flew back to the fire. This time I dipped water from the bath and passed it to Mr. Nakai to throw on the burning woodpile. The blaze, however, was so intense that we could not possibly have extinguished it that way.

I heard voices shouting below, "There's a fire. Fire at the villa!" Suddenly four or five farmers broke through the fence and rushed up to us. It took them just a few minutes to get a relay of buckets going and put out the blaze. If the fire had lasted just a little longer, the flames would have spread to the roof.

"Thank Heavens" was my first thought, but in the next instant I was aghast at the sudden realization of what had caused the fire. It was only then that it occurred to me that the disaster had taken place because the previous night, after I removed the unburned sticks of firewood from the furnace, I had left them next to the woodpile, thinking that they were already out. This discovery made me want to burst into tears. As I stood there rooted to the ground, I heard the girl from the house in front say in a loud voice, "Somebody must have been careless about the furnace. The place is gutted."

The village mayor, the policeman, and the head of the fire brigade were among those who appeared. The mayor asked, with his usual gentle smiling face, "You must have been terribly frightened. How did it happen?"

"It was all my fault. I thought that the firewood had burned out." This was all I could say. The tears came welling up, and I stood there incapable of speech, my eyes on the ground. The thought came to me then that the police might arrest me and drag me off like a criminal, and at the same moment I suddenly became aware of the shamefully disheveled appearance I made as I stood there barefoot in my nightgown. I felt utterly lost.

The mayor quietly asked, in a tone of sympathy, "I understand. Is your mother all right?"

"She is resting in her room. It was a dreadful shock for her."

"Anyway," said the young policeman, trying to comfort me, "it's a good thing that the house didn't catch fire."

Just then Mr. Nakai reappeared, having changed his clothes in the meanwhile, and began to shout all out of breath, "What's all the fuss about? Just a little wood got burned. It never turned into a real fire." He was obviously trying to cover up my stupid mistake.

"I understand perfectly," said the mayor nodding. He spoke for a few minutes with the policeman, then said, "We'll be going now. Please remember me to your mother." They all left except for the policeman, who walked up to me, and in a voice so faint it was only a breathing said, "No report will be made on what happened tonight."

After he had gone Mr. Nakai asked in a tense voice what the policeman had said. I answered, "He told me that they wouldn't make a report." The neighbors who were still standing around apparently caught my words, for they began gradually to drift away, murmuring expressions of relief. Mr. Nakai wished me a good night and started off. Then I stood alone, my mind a blank, by the burned woodpile. In tears I looked up at the sky, and I could see the first traces of the dawn.

I went to wash my hands, feet, and face. Somehow the thought of appearing before Mother frightened me, and I idled around the bathroom, arranging my hair. I went then to the kitchen where I spent the time until it grew light in making a quite unnecessary rearrangement of the cooking utensils.

I tiptoed to Mother's room only to find that she was already completely dressed and seated, looking absolutely exhausted, in an armchair. She smiled when she saw me, but her face was dreadfully pale.

I did not smile in return but stood without a word behind her chair. After a little while, Mother said, "It wasn't anything, was it? Only firewood that was meant to be burned."

I was swept by a wave of happiness. I remembered from childhood Sunday school classes the proverb in the Bible, "A word fitly spoken is like apples of gold in pictures of silver," and I thanked God from the bottom of my heart for my good fortune in having a mother so full of tenderness.

After finishing a light breakfast, I set to work disposing of the burned woodpile. Osaki, the proprietress of the village inn, came trotting up from the garden gate. "What happened? I just heard about it. What happened last night?" Tears shone in her eyes.

"I am sorry," I murmured in apology.

"There's nothing to be sorry about. What about the police?"

"They said it was all right."

"Oh, that's a relief." She looked genuinely glad.

I discussed with Osaki how I should express my thanks and apologies to the village. She was of the opinion that money would be most suitable and suggested the houses I should visit with presents of money and apologies. She added, "If you had rather not make the rounds all by yourself, I'll join you."

"It would be best, wouldn't it, for me to go alone?"

"Can you manage it alone? If you can, it would be."

"I'll go alone."

When I had finished disposing of the wood, I asked Mother for some money, which I wrapped in little packets of 100 yen each. On the outside I wrote the words "With apologies."

I called first at the village hall. The mayor was out, and I gave the packet to the girl at the reception desk saying, "What I did last night was unpardonable, but from now on I shall be most careful. Please forgive me and convey my apologies to the mayor."

I next visited the house of the fire chief. He himself came to the door. He gave me a sad little smile but did not say anything. For some reason, I burst into tears. "Please forgive me for last night." I took a precipitous leave and ran through the streets with the tears pouring down my face. I looked such a fright that I had to go back home to put on some fresh make-up. I was just about to set out again when Mother appeared. "Not finished yet? Where are you going this time?"

"I've only just begun," I answered, not lifting my face.

"It must be a terrible ordeal for you." Mother's tone was warmly understanding. It was her love which gave me the strength to make all the rest of the calls, this time without once weeping.

Wherever I went the people sympathized and attempted to console me. Mr. Nishiyama's young wife —I say young but she's already about forty—was the only one who rebuked me. "Please be careful in the future. You may belong to the nobility, for all I know, but I've been watching with my heart in my mouth the way you two have been living, like children playing house. It's only a miracle you haven't had a fire before, considering the reckless way you live. Please be sure to take the utmost care from now on. If there had been a strong wind last night, the whole village would have gone up in flames."

I felt the truth of Mrs. Nishiyama's accusation. Things were really exactly as she described, and I couldn't dislike her in the least for having scolded me.

Mother had tried to comfort me by making the joke about the firewood being for burning, but supposing there had been a strong wind, the whole village might have burned down, just as Mrs. Nishiyama said. If that had happened, not even my suicide could have served as sufficient apology, and my death would not only have caused Mother's but have blackened forever my Father's name. I know that the aristocracy is now not what it once was, but if it must perish in any case, I would like to see it go down as elegantly as possible. I couldn't rest in my grave if I died in atonement for having started a fire.

I began from the following day to devote my energies to working in the fields. Mr. Nakai's daughter sometimes helps me. Ever since my disgraceful act of having started a fire, I have felt somehow as if the color of my blood has turned a little darker, as if I am becoming every day more of an uncouth country girl. When, for instance, I sit on the porch knitting with Mother, I feel strangely cramped and choked, and it comes as a relief when I go out into the fields to dig the earth.

Manual labor, I suppose one would call it. This is not the first time I've done such work. I was conscripted during the war and even made to do coolie labor. The sneakers I now wear when I work in the fields are the ones the Army issued me. That was the first time in my life I had put such things on my feet, but they were surprisingly comfortable, and when I walked around the garden wearing them I felt as if I could understand the light-heartedness of the bird or animal that walks barefoot on the ground. That is the only pleasant memory I have of the war. What a dreary business the war was.

Last year nothing happened
The year before nothing happened
And the year before that nothing happened.

An amusing poem to this effect appeared in a newspaper just after the war ended. Of course all kinds of things actually did take place, but when I try to recall them now, I experience that same feeling that nothing happened. I hate talking about the war or listening to other people's memories. Many people died, I know, but it was still a dreary business, and it bores me now. I suppose you might say I take a very egocentric view of it. Only when I was conscripted and forced to do coolie labor in sneakers was I able to think of it except in terms of its dreariness. I often had harsh thoughts about the coolie labor, but thanks to it I became quite robust, and even now I sometimes think that if ever I have difficulty in eking out a living, I can always get along by performing manual labor.

One day, about the time that the war was entering

its really desperate phase, a man dressed in a kind of military uniform came to our house in Nishikata Street and handed me conscription papers and a schedule listing the days I was required to work. I discovered that from the following day I would have to report on alternate days at a base in the mountains behind Tachikawa. In spite of myself, I found myself in tears.

"I suppose a substitute wouldn't do?" The tears kept flowing and I had begun to sob.

The man answered firmly, "The Army has work for you, and you yourself must go."

The next day it rained. An officer delivered us a sermon as we stood lined up at the foot of the mountain. "Victory is a certainty," he said by way of preamble. "Victory is a certainty, but unless everybody does exactly what the Army orders, all our plans will be thwarted, and we will have another Okinawa. We want you without fail to do every bit of the work you are given. Next, you are to be on guard against one another. There is no telling whether spies have been planted among you. You will now be working in military positions just like soldiers, and we want you to exercise every possible caution not to reveal to other people under any circumstances what you have seen."

The mountain was smouldering in the rain as we stood there, close to five hundred men and women. We listened with all due reverence to his address, in spite of the drenching rain. The unit also included boys and girls from the elementary schools, all of them with frozen little faces on the verge of tears. The rain went through my coat, penetrated my jacket, and finally soaked through to my underwear.

I spent that whole day carrying baskets of earth on my back. The next time at the base I tugged ropes in a team of laborers. That was the work I liked best.

Two or three times while I was out working in the mountains I had the impression that the schoolboys were staring at me in a most disagreeable manner. I was shouldering baskets of earth one day when a couple of them passed by, and I heard one of them whisper, "Think she's a spy?"

I was astonished. I asked the girl carrying earth next to me what made the boy say such a thing. She answered seriously, "Perhaps because you look like a foreigner."

"Do I? Do you also think I'm a spy?"

"No," she answered, this time with a little smile.

"I am a Japanese," I said and couldn't keep from giggling at the obvious silliness of my own words.

One fine morning which I had spent hauling logs along with the men, the young officer suddenly frowned and pointed at me. "Hey you. You, come here."

He walked quickly toward the pine forest, and I followed him, my heart pounding with nervousness and fear. He stopped by a pile of timber just brought from the saw mill, and turned around to me. "It must be very hard working that way every day. Today please just watch over this lumber." He spoke with a smile, flashing his white teeth.

"You mean I should stand here?"

"It's cool and quiet, and you can take a nap on top of the pile. If you get bored, perhaps you'd like to read this." He took a small volume from his pocket and tossed it shyly on the boards. "It isn't much of a book, but please read it if you like."

It was called *Troika*. I picked it up. "Thank you very much. There's someone in my family also who likes books, but he's in the South Pacific now."

He misunderstood. "Oh, your husband. South Pacific. That's terrible." He shook his head in sympathy. "At any rate, today you stand guard duty. I'll bring your lunch box myself later on. You just rest without worrying about anything." With these words, he strode off rapidly.

I sat on the lumber pile and began to read the book. I had read about half when the crunching of his boots announced the officer's return. "I have brought your lunch. It must be very tedious being here alone." He deposited the lunch box on the grass and hurried off again.

When I had finished the lunch, I crawled up on

top of the lumber pile and stretched out to read the book. I read the whole thing through and nodded off. I woke after three with the sudden impression that I had seen the young officer before, but where I could not recall. I clambered down from the pile and was just smoothing down my hair when I heard the crunching of his boots again.

"Thank you very much for having come today. You may leave now if you wish."

I ran up to him and held out the book. I wanted to express my thanks, but the words did not come. In silence I looked at his face, and when our eyes met, mine filled with tears. Then tears shone also in his.

We parted without words, just like that, and the young officer never again appeared at the place where I worked. That was the only day I was able to take it easy. From then on I went every other day to Tachikawa to do my stint of hard labor. Mother worried a great deal about my health, but the work actually made me stronger than ever before, and even now I am, at least, a woman who is not particularly distressed even by the hardest labor in the fields.

I said that I hate to discuss the war or hear about it, but now I find I have told all about my "precious experience." But that's about the only memory of the war I ever feel the slightest inclination to relate. The rest might aptly be summed up by the poem:

Last year nothing happened
The year before nothing happened
And the year before that nothing happened.

Idiotically enough, all that remains of my war experiences is the pair of sneakers.

The mention of the sneakers took me off again on another digression, but I should add that although wearing what may be called my unique memento of the war and going out into the fields every day helps to relieve the secret anxiety and uneasiness deep in my heart, Mother has of late been growing weaker day by day.

The snake eggs.

The fire.

Mother's health has shockingly deteriorated while I, quite on the contrary, feel as though I am steadily turning into a coarse, low-class woman. I can't escape the feeling that it is by sucking the life-breath out of Mother that I am fattening.

Mother has never said a word concerning the fire except for her joke about the firewood being for burning. Far from reprimanding me, she seemed to pity me, but the shock she received was certainly ten times as great as mine. Ever since the fire Mother sometimes groans in her sleep, and on nights when a strong wind is blowing, she slips out of bed any number of times, however late it may be, and goes around the house making sure that everything is all right. She never looks well. Some days even walking seems a great strain for her. She had expressed a desire to help me in the fields, and although I had discouraged her, she insisted on carrying five or six great bucketfuls of water from the well. The next day her back was so stiff she could barely breathe. She spent the day in bed. After that she appeared to have given up the idea of manual labor. Once in a while she walks out into the fields but only to observe intently what I am doing.

Today, while Mother was watching me work, she suddenly remarked, "They say that people who like summer flowers die in the summer. I wonder if it's true." I did not answer but went on watering the eggplants. It is already the beginning of summer. She continued softly, "I am very fond of hibiscus, but we haven't a single one in this garden."

"We have plenty of oleanders," I answered in an intentionally sharp tone.

"I don't like them. I like almost all summer flowers, but oleanders are too loud."

"I like roses best. But they bloom in all four seasons. I wonder if people who like roses best have to die four times over again."

We both laughed.

"Won't you rest a bit?" Mother asked, still smiling. She added, "I have something I'd like to talk over with you today."

"What is it? If it's about your dying, no thanks."

I followed Mother to a bench under the wisteria trellis. The wisteria blossoms were at their end, and the soft afternoon sunlight filtering through the leaves fell on our laps and dyed them green.

"There's something I've been meaning to tell you for quite a while, but I was waiting for a moment when we were both in a good mood. You see, it's not a very easy thing to discuss. But today I feel somehow as if I can talk about it. I ask you please to restrain yourself and listen until I have finished. The truth is that Naoji is alive."

I stiffened all over.

"Five or six days ago I had a letter from your Uncle Wada. It seems that a man who used to work for him has recently returned from the South Pacific. He went to your uncle's office to pay his respects, and then, quite by accident, it came out that he had been in the same unit with Naoji and that Naoji is safe and will soon be returning. He had one unpleasant thing to report. According to this man, Naoji has become a rather serious opium addict."

"Again!"

My mouth twisted as if I had eaten something bitter. When Naoji was in high school, in imitation of a certain novelist, he had taken to drugs, and he finally ran up such an enormous bill at the pharmacist's that it had taken Mother two years to pay it in full.

"Yes. He seems to have taken it up again. But the man said that he's certain to be cured by the time he gets back because they won't let him return otherwise. Your uncle's letter goes on to say that even if Naoji is cured when he returns there's no immediate likelihood of finding a job for someone in his frame of mind. Even perfectly normal people become rather peculiar nowadays if they work in Tokyo—what with all the confusion—and a semi-invalid who has just recovered from narcotic poisoning might go berserk in no time. There's no telling what he might do. If Naoji comes back, the best thing would be for us to take care of him here in the mountains for the time being and not let him go anywhere else. That's one thing. And, Kazuko, your uncle had another thing in his letter. He says that our money is all gone, and what with the blocking of savings and the capital levy, he won't be able to send us as much as he has before. It will be extremely difficult for him to manage our living expenses, especially when Naoji arrives and there are three of us to take care of. He suggests that we should waste no time in finding for you either a husband or else a position in some household."

"As a servant?"

"No, your uncle wrote that he knew of a family that's related to us and in the peerage where you could have a position as governess to the little girls. That probably wouldn't be too depressing or awkward for you."

"I wonder if there isn't some other job."

"He says that any other profession would be impractical for you."

"Why impractical?"

Mother smiled sadly but did not answer.

"No! I've had enough of such talk!" I burst out hysterically, knowing even as I did so that I would regret it. But I couldn't stop. "Look at me in these wretched sneakers—look!" I was crying, but I brushed the tears away with the back of my hand and looked Mother in the face. A voice within me repeated, "I mustn't, I mustn't," but words, having no connection with my expressed self, poured forth, as if from the depths of my subconscious.

"Didn't you once say that it was because of me, because you had me, that you were going to Izu? Didn't you say that if you didn't have me you would die? That's why I've stayed here without budging from your side. And here I am wearing these sneakers because my only thought has been to grow vegetables you would like. Now you hear that Naoji's coming home, and suddenly you find me in the way. 'Go off and become a servant!' you say. It's too much, too much."

My words seemed horrible even to myself, but they could not be stopped, as if they had an existence of their own.

"If we're poor and our money's gone, why don't we sell all our expensive clothes? Why don't we sell this house? I can do something. I can get a job working at the village office, and if they won't hire me there, I can do coolie work. Poverty is nothing. As long as you love me, all I want is to spend my whole life by your side. But you love Naoji more than you love me, don't you? I'll go. I'll go. I've never been able to get along with Naoji and it would only bring unhappiness to all three of us if I stayed. We've lived together for a long time, and I have nothing to regret in our relationship. Now you and Naoji can stay together, just the two of you. I hope for your sake he'll be a very good son to you. I'm sick of it. I'm sick of this life. I'll go. I'll leave today, at once. I have somewhere I can go."

I stood up.

"Kazuko!" Mother spoke severely. Her face was filled with a dignity she had never shown me before. When she stood and confronted me, she looked almost taller than I.

I wanted to beg her pardon, but the words would not come from my mouth. Instead I uttered quite different ones. "You've deceived me. Mother, you've deceived me. You were using me until Naoji came. I've been your servant, and now that you no longer need me you're sending me away."

I let out a cry and burst into tears.

"You are very foolish." Mother's voice as she spoke these words was shaking with anger.

I lifted my head. "Yes, I am. I've been taken advantage of because I'm a fool. You're getting rid of me because I'm a fool. It's best I go, isn't it? Poverty —what's that? Money—what's that? I don't understand such things. I had always believed in love, in my mother's love, in that at least."

Again I spoke in that stupid, unforgivable way.

Mother turned her head away abruptly. She was weeping. I wanted to beg her pardon and to cling to her, but my hands were dirty from my work in the fields, and this involuntary embarrassment kept me distant. "Everything will be all right if I'm not here. I'll go. I have somewhere I can go."

With these words I ran off to the bathroom where I washed my face and hands, still sobbing. I went to my room, changed my clothes, only once again to be overcome with weeping. I wanted to weep more, more, until I had drained every tear from my body. I ran to the foreign-style room on the second floor, threw myself on the bed, and covering my head in the blankets, wept my very flesh away. Then my mind began to wander aimlessly. Gradually out of my grief, the desire for a certain person crystallized in me, and I yearned unbearably to see his face, to hear his voice. I had that very particular sensation one experiences when the doctor prescribes cauterization of the soles of one's feet, and one must bear the pain without flinching.

Toward evening Mother came softly into the room and switched on the light. She approached the bed and called my name in a very gentle voice.

I got up and sat on the bed, sweeping both hands over my hair. I looked at her face and smiled.

Mother also smiled faintly and then sank into the sofa under the window. "I have just disobeyed your uncle for the first time in my life. I wrote a letter in answer to his, requesting him to leave my children's affairs to me. Kazuko, we'll sell our clothes. We'll sell our clothes one after another and use the money just as we please, for whatever useless things we feel like. Let's live extravagantly. I don't want to let you work in the fields any more. Let's buy our vegetables even if they are expensive. It's unreasonable to expect you to spend every day working like a farmer."

To tell the truth, the strain of daily work in the fields had begun to take its toll. I am sure that the reason why I wept and stormed as if I had gone off my head was that the combination of physical exhaustion and my unhappiness had made me hate and resent everything.

I sat on the bed in silence, my eyes averted.

"Kazuko."

"Yes."

"What did you mean by saying that you had somewhere to go?"

I could tell that I had turned red to the nape of my neck.

"Mr. Hosoda?"

I did not answer.

Mother gave a great sigh. "May I bring up something that happened a long time ago?"

"Please do," I whispered.

"When you left your husband and returned to the house in Nishikata Street, I did not intend to say a word of reproach, but there was one thing that made me say that you had betrayed me. Do you remember? You burst into tears and I realized that I had been wrong to say such a terrible thing."

But my memory was that I had felt grateful to Mother at the time for talking to me in such a way, and my tears had been of happiness.

"When I said that you had betrayed me it was not because you left your husband's house. It was because I had learned from him that you and that painter Hosoda were lovers. That news came as a terrible shock. Mr. Hosoda had already been a married man for years and had children. I knew it could never come to anything, no matter how much you loved him."

"Lovers—what a thing to say. It was nothing but groundless suspicion on my husband's part."

"Perhaps. I don't suppose you can still be thinking of Mr. Hosoda. Where was it then that you meant when you said you had somewhere to go?"

"Not to Mr. Hosoda's."

"Really? Then where?"

"Mother, recently I have discovered the one way in which human beings differ completely from other animals. Man has, I know, language, knowledge, principles, and social order, but don't all the other animals have them too, granted the difference of degree? Perhaps the animals even have religions. Man boasts of being the lord of all creation, but it would seem as if essentially he does not differ in the least from other animals. But, Mother, there was one way I thought of. Perhaps you won't understand. It's a faculty absolutely unique to man—having secrets. Can you see what I mean?"

Mother blushed faintly and gave a charming smile. "If your secrets only bear good fruit, it will be all I could ask. Every morning I pray to your father's spirit to make you happy."

Suddenly there flashed across my mind an image of driving with Father through Nasuno and getting out on the way, and how the autumn fields looked. The autumn flowers—asters, pinks, gentians, valerians—were all in bloom. The wild grapes were still green.

Later Father and I boarded a motorboat at Lake Biwa. I jumped into the water. The little fish that live in the weeds brushed against my legs, and the shadow of my legs, distinctly reflected on the bottom of the lake, moved with me. The picture bore no relation to what Mother and I had been discussing, but it flashed into my mind, only to vanish.

I slid off the bed and threw my arms around Mother's knees. "Mother, please forgive me." I was at last able to say it.

Those days, as I remember them now, were the last in which the dying embers of our happiness still glowed. Once Naoji returned from the South Pacific, our real hell began.

夕
顔

CHAPTER THREE / MOONFLOWERS

A sensation of helplessness, as if it were utterly impossible to go on living. Painful waves beat relentlessly on my heart, as after a thunderstorm the white clouds frantically scud across the sky. A terrible emotion—shall I call it an apprehension—wrings my heart only to release it, makes my pulse falter, and chokes my breath. At times everything grows misty and dark before my eyes, and I feel that the strength of my whole body is oozing away through my finger tips.

Of late a gloomy rain has been falling almost incessantly. Whatever I do depresses me. Today I took a wicker chair out onto the porch, intending to work again on the sweater which I began to knit this spring. The wool is of a somewhat faded rose, and I am eking it out with cobalt-blue yarn to make a sweater. The pale rose wool originally came from a scarf that Mother knitted for me twenty years ago, when I was still in elementary school. The end of the scarf was formed into a kind of skullcap, and when I put it on and looked at myself in the mirror, a little imp stared back at me. The scarf was very different in color from the scarves my school friends wore, and that fact alone sufficed to make me loathe it with an unreasoning fury. I felt so ashamed to be seen in it that I had refused to wear it again, and for years it had lain hidden away in a drawer somewhere. This spring it came to light, and I unraveled it. I decided to make it into a sweater for myself, in the pious intention of resuscitating a dead possession. But somehow the faded color failed to interest me, and I had put the yarn aside again. Today, having nothing else to do, I took it out on the spur of the moment and idly began to knit. It was only while I was knitting that I realized the pale rose of the wool and the grey of the overcast sky were blending into one, making a harmony of colors so soft and mild that no words could describe it. I had never suspected that the important thing was to consider the match a costume makes with the color of the sky. What a beautiful, wonderful thing color harmony is, I thought to myself, rather surprised. It is amazing how when one unites the grey of the sky with the pale rose of the wool, both colors at once come alive. The wool I held in my hands became vibrant with warmth, and the cold rainy sky was soft as velvet. I remembered a Monet painting of a cathedral in the mist, and I felt as if, thanks to the wool, I had for the first time understood what good taste is. Good taste. Mother had chosen the pale rose wool because she knew just how lovely it would look against the snowy winter sky, but in my foolishness I had disliked it. I had had my own way, for Mother never attempted to force anything on me. During all this time Mother had not said a word of explanation but had waited these twenty years until I was able to appreciate the beauty of the color myself. I thought what a wonderful Mother I had. At the same moment clouds of dread and apprehension suddenly welled up within my breast as I wondered whether Naoji and I between us had not tortured and weakened Mother to the point of killing her. The more I reflected the more certain it seemed that the future had in store for us only horrible, evil things. The thought filled me with such nameless fears that I felt almost incapable of going on living. The strength left my fingers, and I dropped my knitting needles on my lap. A great sigh shook me. With my eyes still shut, I lifted my head. Before I knew what I was doing, I had cried, "Mother!"

"Yes?" Mother, leaning over a desk in a corner of

the room, reading a book, answered with a note of doubt in her voice.

I was confused. In an unnecessarily loud voice I declared, "The roses have bloomed at last. Did you know it, Mother? I just noticed it now. They've bloomed at last."

The roses in front of the porch had been brought back long ago by Uncle Wada from France—or was it England? at any rate some distant country—and had now been transplanted here from our house in Nishikata Street. I had been fully aware this morning that one of them had bloomed, but to cover my embarrassment I pretended with exaggerated enthusiasm just to have discovered the fact. The flowers, of a dark purple, had a sombre pride and strength.

"Yes, I knew," Mother said gently, adding, "Such things seem very important to you."

"Perhaps. Are you sorry for me?"

"No. I only meant to say that it was typical of you. It's just like you to paste pictures by Renoir on the kitchen match boxes or to make handkerchiefs for dolls. To hear you talk about the roses in the garden, one would think you were discussing live people."

"That's because I haven't any children."

I was quite taken aback by my own remark. I nervously fingered the knitting on my lap. It was as if I clearly could hear a man's voice, a scratchy bass, like a voice on the telephone, saying, "What do you expect —she's twenty-nine!" My cheeks burned with shame.

Mother made no comment but went back to her book. For some days now she has been wearing a gauze mask over her mouth, and that may have been the cause of her exceptional taciturnity of late. She wore the mask in obedience to Naoji's instructions.

Naoji had returned a week or so before from the South Pacific, his face sallow. One summer evening, without a word of warning, he had burst into the garden, slamming the wooden gate behind him. "What a horror! What atrocious taste for a house! You should put out a sign 'China Mansions: Chow Mein'!"

These were Naoji's words of greeting on first seeing me.

Mother had taken to bed two or three days before with a pain in her tongue. I could not detect anything abnormal about the tip of her tongue, but she said that the slightest movement hurt her unbearably. At meal times she could only get down a thin soup. I suggested that the doctor examine her, but Mother shook her head and said with a forced smile, "He would only laugh at me." I painted her tongue with Lugol, but it had no apparent effect. Mother's illness unnerved me.

Just at this juncture, Naoji came.

He sat for a moment by Mother's pillow and inclined his head in a word of greeting. That was all—

he immediately sprang to his feet and rushed off to inspect the house. I followed behind him.

"How do you find Mother? Changed?"

"She's changed all right. She's grown thin. It'd be best for her if she died soon. People like Mama are not meant to go on living in such a world as this. She was too pathetic even for me to look at her."

"How about me?"

"You've coarsened. Your face looks as if you've got two or three men. Is there any saké? Tonight I'm going to get drunk."

I went to the village inn and begged the proprietress to let me have a little saké, in honor of my brother's return, but I was told that they were unfortunately just out of stock. When I repeated this information to Naoji, his face darkened into an expression the like of which I never before had seen, and which made him a stranger. "Damn it! You don't know how to deal with her." He got me to tell him where the inn was and rushed out. That was that. I waited for hours for his return, but in vain. I had made baked apples, one of Naoji's favorite dishes, and an omelette, and had even put brighter electric lights in the dining-room to add some cheer. While I was waiting, Osaki, the girl from the inn, put her head in at the kitchen door and whispered urgently, "Excuse me. Is it all right? He's drinking gin." Her pop-eyes bulged even more than usual.

"Gin? You mean methyl alcohol?"

"No, it's not methyl, but just the same. . . ."

"It won't make him sick if he drinks it, will it?"

"No, but still. . . ."

"Let him drink it then."

Osaki nodded as if she were swallowing and went away.

I reported to Mother, "He's drinking at Osaki's place."

Mother twisted her mouth a little into a smile. "He must have given up opium. Please finish the dinner. Tonight we'll all three sleep in this room. Put Naoji's bedding in the middle."

I felt as if I could weep.

Naoji returned late that night, thumping loudly through the house. The large, room-size mosquito net was spread open, and the three of us crept inside.

Lying there I asked him, "Why don't you tell Mother something about the South Seas?"

"There's nothing to tell. Nothing at all. I've forgotten. When I returned to Japan and got on the train the rice fields looked unbelievably beautiful from the train window. That's all. Turn out the light. I can't sleep."

I turned out the light. The summer moonlight flooded into the mosquito netting.

The next morning Naoji, lying in bed and smoking a cigarette, looked out at the sea in the distance.

"I hear your tongue hurts you." He spoke as if he had noticed for the first time that Mother was not well.

Mother merely smiled feebly.

"I'm sure it's psychological. You probably sleep at night with your mouth open. Very careless of you. You should wear a gauze mask. Soak some gauze in Rivanol solution and put it inside a mask."

I exploded, "What kind of treatment do you call that?"

"It's called the aesthetic treatment."

"But I'm sure that Mother would hate wearing a mask."

Mother dislikes putting anything on her face, even glasses or an eye-patch if her eyelids are inflamed, let alone a mask.

I asked, "Mother, will you wear one?"

"Yes, I will." Her voice was earnest. I was quite taken aback. Mother was apparently resolved to believe and obey anything that Naoji said.

After breakfast I soaked some gauze in Rivanol solution, as Naoji had directed, folded it into a mask, and took it to Mother. She accepted it without a word and meekly tied the strings around her ears. She looked as she lay there pathetically like a little girl.

That afternoon Naoji announced that he would have to go to Tokyo to see his friends. He changed to a business suit and set off with 2,000 yen from Mother.

Almost ten days have gone by since his departure, and as yet there is no sign when he will return. Every day Mother wears her mask and waits for Naoji. She has told me that the medicine is very effective and that wearing the mask greatly relieves the pain in her tongue. I can't help feeling, however, that Mother is not telling the truth. She is out of bed now, but her appetite remains poor and she seldom speaks. I am worried about her, and I wonder what can be keeping Naoji so long. No doubt he is amusing himself with that novelist Uehara and is at this moment being sucked into the frenzied whirlpool of Tokyo. The more I let my thoughts run along such lines the bitterer my life seems. It is a sure indication that I am at last losing control of myself when I burst out for no good reason with a report on the activities of the roses or mention the fact I haven't any children—lapses I would never have believed myself capable of.

My knitting fell as I stood up with a cry of dismay. I felt at an utter loss what to do with myself. With shaking limbs, I climbed the stairs to the foreign-style room on the second floor.

This is to be Naoji's room. Four or five days ago Mother and I settled this, and I asked Mr. Nakai to help me move in Naoji's wardrobe and bookcases, five or six wooden crates stuffed with books and papers, and various other objects—in short, everything that had been in his room in our old house in

Nishikata Street. We decided to await his return from Tokyo before we put the wardrobe and bookcases in place, not knowing where he would like them. The room was so cluttered that there was scarcely space enough to turn around. Aimlessly I picked up one of Naoji's notebooks from an open crate. The words "Moonflower Journal" were written on the cover. The notebook seems to have been kept while Naoji was suffering from narcotic poisoning.

A sensation of burning to death. And excruciating though it is, I cannot pronounce even the simple words "it hurts." Do not try to shrug off this portent of a hell unparalleled, unique in the history of man, bottomless!

Philosophy? Lies. Principles? Lies. Ideals? Lies. Order? Lies. Sincerity? Truth? Purity? All lies. They say the wisteria of Ushijima are a thousand years old, and the wisteria of Kumano date from centuries ago. I have heard that wisteria clusters at Ushijima attain a maximum length of nine feet, and those at Kumano of over five feet. My heart dances only in those clusters of wisteria blossom.

That too is somebody's child. It is alive.

Logic, inevitably, is the love of logic. It is not the love for living human beings.

Money and women. Logic, intimidated, scampers off precipitously.

The courageous testimony of Dr. Faust that a maiden's smile is more precious than history, philosophy, education, religion, law, politics, economics, and all the other branches of learning.

Learning is another name for vanity. It is the effort of human beings not to be human beings.

I can swear even before Goethe that I am a superbly gifted writer. Flawless construction, the proper leavening of humor, pathos to bring tears to the reader's eyes—or else a distinguished novel, perfect of its kind, to be read aloud sonorously with the deference due it, this (shall I call it running commentary on a film?) I claim I could write were I not ashamed. There's something fundamentally cheap about such awareness of genius. Only a madman would read a novel with deference. In that case it had best be done in formal clothes, like going to a funeral. So long as it does not seem as affected as a good work! I will write my novel clumsily, deliberately making a botch of it, just to see a smile of genuine pleasure on my friend's face—to fall on my bottom and patter off scratching my head. Oh, to see my friend's happy face!

What is this affection which would make me blow the toy bugle of bad prose and bad character to proclaim, "Here is the greatest fool in Japan! Compared to me, you're all right—be of good health!"

Friend! You who relate with a smug face, "That's his bad habit, what a pity!" You do not know that you are loved.

I wonder if there is anyone who is not depraved.

A wearisome thought.

I want money.

Unless I have it. . . .

In my sleep, a natural death!

I have run up a debt of close to a thousand yen with the pharmacist. Today I surreptitiously introduced a clerk from the pawnshop into the house and ushered him to my room. I asked, "Is anything here valuable enough to pawn? If there is, take it away. I am in desperate need of money."

The clerk, with scarcely a glance at the room, had the effrontery to say, "Why don't you forget the whole idea? After all, the furniture doesn't belong to you."

"Very well!" I said with animation, "just take the things I have bought with my own pocket money." But not a one of all the odds and ends I piled before him had any value as a pledge.

Item. A hand in plaster. This was the right hand of Venus. A hand like a dahlia blossom, a pure white hand, mounted on a stand. But if you looked at it carefully you could tell how this pure white, delicate hand, with whorl-less finger tips and unmarked palms, expressed, so pitifully that even the beholder was stabbed with pain, the shame intense enough to make Venus stop her breath; in the gesture was implicit the moment when Venus' full nakedness was seen by a man, when she twisted away her body, flushed all over with the prickling warmth of her shock, the whirlwind of her shame, and the tragedy of her nudity. Unfortunately, this was only a piece of bric-à-brac. *The clerk valued it at fifty sen.*

Items. A large map of the suburbs of Paris. A celluloid top almost a foot in diameter. A special pen-point with which one can write letters finer than threads. All things bought by me under the impression that they were great bargains.

The clerk laughed and said, "I must be leaving now."

"Wait!" I cried, holding him back. I finally managed to load him down with an immense stack of books for which he gave me five yen. The books on my shelves were, with a few exceptions, cheap paper-bound editions, and at that I had bought them second-hand. It was not surprising that they fetched so little.

To settle a debt of a thousand yen—five yen. That is approximately my effective strength. It is no laughing matter.

But rather than the patronizing "But being decadent is the only way to survive!" of some who criticize me, I would far prefer to be told simply to go and die. It's straightforward. But people almost never say, "Die!" Paltry, prudent hypocrites!

Justice? That's not where you'll find the so-called class struggle. Humanity? Don't be silly. I know. It is knocking down your fellow-men for the sake of your own happiness. It is a killing. What meaning has it unless there is a verdict of "Die!" It's no use cheating.

There aren't any decent people in our class either. Idiots, specters, penny-pinchers, mad dogs, braggarts, high-flown words, piss from above the clouds.

"Die!" Just to be vouchsafed that word would be far more than I deserve.

The war. Japan's war is an act of desperation.

To die by being sucked into an act of desperation . . . no thanks. I had rather die by my own hand.

People always make a serious face when they tell a lie. The seriousness of our leaders these days! Pooh!

I want to spend my time with people who don't look to be respected. But such good people won't want to spend their time with me.

When I pretended to be precocious, people started the rumor that I was precocious. When I acted like an idler, rumor had it I was an idler. When I pretended I couldn't write a novel, people said I couldn't write. When I acted like a liar, they called me a liar. When I acted like a rich man, they started the rumor I was rich. When I feigned indifference, they classed me as the indifferent type. But when I inadvertently groaned because I was really in pain, they started the rumor that I was faking suffering.

The world is out of joint.

Doesn't that mean in effect that I have no choice but suicide?

In spite of my suffering, at the thought that I was sure to end up by killing myself, I cried aloud and burst into tears.

There is the story of how on a morning in spring as the sun shone on a branch of plum where two or three blossoms had opened, a young student of Heidelberg was dangling from the branch, dead.

"Mama, scold me please!"

"What for?"

"They say I'm a weakling."

"Do they? A weakling. . . . I don't think I need scold you about that any more."

Mama's goodness is unsurpassed. Whenever I

think of her, I want to cry. I will die by way of apology to Mama.

Please forgive me. Just this once, please forgive me.

(New Year's Poem)
The years!
Still quite blind
The little stork-chicks
Are growing up.
Ah! how they fatten!

Morphine, atromol, narcopon, philipon, pantopon, pabinal, panopin, atropin.

What is self-esteem? Self-esteem!

It is impossible for a human being—no, a man—to go on living without thinking "I am one of the élite," "I have my good points," etc.

I detest people, am detested by them.

Test of wits.

Solemnity=feeling of idiocy.

Anyway, you can be sure of one thing, a man's got to fake just to stay alive.

A letter requesting a loan:

"Your answer.

Please answer.

And in such a way that it will be good tidings for me.

I am moaning to myself in the expectation of humiliations of every sort.

I am not putting on an act. Absolutely not.

I beg it of you.

I feel as if I will die of shame.

I am not exaggerating.

Every day, every day, I wait for your answer; night and day I tremble all over.

Do not make me eat dirt.

I can hear a smothered laugh from the walls. Late at night I toss in my bed.

Do not humiliate me.

My sister!"

Having read that much, I shut the "Moonflower Journal" and returned it to the wooden crate. I walked to the window, threw it open, and looking down on the garden smoky with white rain, I remembered the events of those days.

Six years have already passed since then. Naoji's drug addiction eventually led to my divorce. No, I shouldn't say that. I have the feeling that my divorce was settled from the moment I was born, that even if Naoji had not been addicted to drugs the divorce would have occurred sooner or later for some other cause. Naoji was in difficulties about paying the pharmacist and frequently importuned me for money. I had just been married and could not be entirely free about money. Besides, I felt strongly that it was most improper for me to slip furtively into the hands of my brother money I had received from my husband. After talking the matter over with my maid Oseki, who had come with me from my mother's house, I decided to sell my bracelets, necklaces, and dresses. Naoji had sent me a letter concluding, "I feel such anguish and shame that I can't bear to meet you or even to talk to you over the telephone. Please send the money with Oseki to the apartment [he gave the address] of the novelist Uehara Jirō, whom I'm sure you must know, at least by name. Mr. Uehara has the reputation of being an evil man, but he is not actually like that at all, and there is no need to worry about sending me the money at his address. I have arranged with Uehara to let me know immediately by telephone when the money arrives, so please do it that way. I want to keep my addiction from Mama, at least. Somehow I intend to cure myself before she learns of it. If I get the money from you this time, I will pay back the pharmacist all that I owe him. I may go afterward to our villa in the mountains to recuperate. I really mean it. The day I pay back my whole debt I intend to give up drugs completely. I swear it to God. Please believe me. Please keep it a secret from Mama, and send the money to Mr. Uehara's."

That is more or less what was in the letter. I followed his directions and had Oseki take the money secretly to Mr. Uehara's apartment, but the promise in Naoji's letter was, as always, false. He didn't go to the villa to recuperate. Instead, his drug taking seems to have turned into a kind of poisoning and grown steadily more serious. The style of the letters he sent imploring me for money took on an anguished tone which was all but a shriek. Each time I read his words "I promise to give up drugs now," followed by an oath so heart-rending that it made me want to turn my face away from the paper, I realized perfectly well that he might be lying again, but I would nevertheless send Oseki out to sell a piece of jewelry and to take the money to Mr. Uehara.

"What sort of man is Mr. Uehara?"

"He's a short, dark, disagreeable man," Oseki answered, adding, "but he's seldom at home when I call. Usually there's just his wife and a little girl about six years old. His wife is not particularly pretty, but she seems a sweet, intelligent person. You don't have to worry about entrusting your money to a lady like her."

If you were to compare what I was like then to

what I am like now—no, I was so different that no comparison is possible—I had my head in the clouds and was always very easy-going. All the same, I began to be terribly worried what with one sum of money after another being extorted from me, and the whole thing gradually assumed the proportions of a nightmare. One day, returning from the theatre, I sent back the car and walked by myself to Mr. Uehara's apartment.

Mr. Uehara was alone in his room reading a newspaper. He was dressed in a Japanese costume which made him look old and young at the same time. I received a strange first impression as if from a rare beast that I had never before seen.

"My wife has gone with the child to collect the rations." His voice was slightly nasal, and he clipped his words. He seemed to have mistaken me for a friend of his wife's. When I told him that I was Naoji's sister, Mr. Uehara barked a laugh. A cold shiver went through me; I don't know why.

"Shall we go out?" Scarcely had he uttered these words than he threw on a cloak, stepped into a new pair of sandals, and dashed out ahead of me into the hallway.

An early winter's evening. The wind was icy. It felt as if it were blowing in from the river. Mr. Uehara walked in silence, his right shoulder slightly raised as if against the wind. I followed behind him, half running.

We entered the basement of a building behind the Tokyo Theatre. Four or five groups of customers were sitting around tables in a long narrow room, quietly drinking.

Mr. Uehara drank his saké from a tumbler, instead of the usual little cup. He asked them to bring another glass and offered me some. I drank two glassfuls but did not feel anything.

Mr. Uehara drank and smoked, still without uttering a word. This was the first time in my life that I had ever come to such a place, but I felt quite at home and rather happy.

"Liquor would be better, but still. . . ."

"Excuse me?"

"I mean, your brother. It would be a good thing if he switched to some kind of alcohol. I was once a dope addict myself, a long time ago, and I know what a poor view people take of it. Alcohol is the same sort of thing, but about that they're surprisingly indulgent. I think I'll make an alcoholic of your brother. How does that suit you?"

"I once saw an alcoholic. I was about to set out on New Year's calls when I noticed a friend of our chauffeur's with a hideously red face asleep in the car and snoring loudly. I was so surprised that I screamed.

The driver told me the man was a hopeless alcoholic. He dragged the man out of the car and slung him over his shoulders. The man's body flopped about as if he hadn't any bones, and all the while he kept mumbling something. That was the first time I ever saw an alcoholic. It was fascinating."

"I'm also an alcoholic, you know."

"Oh, but not the same kind, are you?"

"And so are you, an alcoholic."

"No, that isn't true. I've seen a real alcoholic, and it's entirely different."

Mr. Uehara for the first time gave a genuine smile. "Then perhaps your brother won't be able to become an alcoholic either, but at least it would be a good idea for him to take up drinking. Let's go. You don't want to be late, do you?"

"It doesn't make any difference."

"To tell the truth, this place is too crowded for me. Waitress! The bill."

"Is it very expensive? If it isn't too much, I have a little money with me."

"In that case, you take care of the bill."

"There may not be enough." I looked inside my bag and told Mr. Uehara how much money I had.

"With that much you have enough to drink at two or three more places. Don't be silly." He spoke with a scowl, then laughed.

"Would you like to go drinking somewhere else?"

He shook his head. "No, I've had enough. I'll get a taxi for you. You had better go back."

We climbed up the dark stairs from the basement. Mr. Uehara, who was one step ahead of me, turned around suddenly and gave me a quick kiss. I took his kiss with my lips tightly shut. I felt no special attraction for him, but all the same, from that moment on my "secret" came into being. Mr. Uehara clattered up the stairs, and I slowly followed, with a strangely transparent feeling. When I stepped outside, the wind from the river felt wonderful against my cheek.

He hailed a taxi for me, and we separated without saying anything.

I felt, as I was tossed in the decrepit old taxi, as if the world had suddenly opened wide as the sea.

One day, when I was feeling depressed after a quarrel with my husband, I suddenly took it in my head to say, "I have a lover."

"I know. It's Hosoda, isn't it? Can't you possibly give him up?"

I remained silent.

Whenever there was any unpleasantness between my husband and myself, this matter would always be brought up. "It's all over now," I thought. It was like buying the wrong material for a dress—once you have cut it you can't sew the material together again, and you'd best throw the whole thing away and start afresh on another piece of material.

One night my husband asked me if the child I was carrying was Hosoda's. I was so frightened that I shook all over. I realize now that my husband and I were both very young. I did not know what love was. I did not even understand simple affection. I was so wild about Mr. Hosoda's pictures that I used to tell people I met that every day of one's life would be filled with beauty if one were the wife of such a man, and that marriage was meaningless unless it were to a man with taste like his. And so everyone misunderstood, and I, who knew nothing of love or affection, would publicly say without any embarrassment that I loved Mr. Hosoda. I never attempted to take back my words, which made things terribly complicated. That was why even the little infant then sleeping within me became the object of my husband's suspicions. Although neither of us openly spoke of divorce, the atmosphere grew increasingly chilly, and I returned to my mother's house. The child was stillborn. I took ill and was confined to my bed. My relations with my husband had come to an end.

Naoji, perhaps feeling a kind of responsibility for my divorce, bellowed that he would die, and his face decomposed with weeping. I asked him how much he still owed the pharmacist. He mentioned a fantastically large figure. Later I learned that Naoji had lied, being unable to confess the actual amount, which was close to three times what he told me.

I said, "I've met your Mr. Uehara. He's a delightful man. Don't you think it would be amusing if the three of us went drinking together sometime? I was simply amazed how cheap saké is. As long as you stick to saké, I can always foot the bill. And don't worry about paying the pharmacist. It will be arranged somehow."

Naoji seemed enchanted that I had met and liked Mr. Uehara. That night, as soon as he had obtained money from me, he rushed off to Mr. Uehara's place.

Addiction is perhaps a sickness of the spirit. I praised Mr. Uehara and borrowed his novels from my brother. When I had read them, I told Naoji what a wonderful writer I thought Mr. Uehara. Naoji was astonished that I could understand him, but seemed very pleased all the same, and made me read other works by Mr. Uehara. Before I knew it I had begun to read his novels in earnest, and Naoji and I gossiped a great deal about him. Naoji staggered off almost every night to drinking parties at Mr. Uehara's. Bit by bit, as Mr. Uehara had planned, Naoji was switching to alcohol. Without Naoji's knowledge, I asked Mother what to do about the pharmacist's bill. She covered her face with one hand and for a while sat motionless. Presently she looked up and said with a smile, "I can't think of anything to do. I don't know how many years it may take, but we'll have to pay back a little each month."

Six years have gone by since then.

Moonflowers. Yes, it must have been painful for Naoji, too. Even now his path is blocked, and he probably still has no idea what to do in what way. His drinking every day must be only in the hope of death.

I wonder how it would be if I let go and yielded myself to real depravity. Perhaps that might make things easier for Naoji.

"I wonder if there is anyone who is not depraved" Naoji wrote in his notebook. Those words made me feel depraved myself, and my uncle and even Mother somehow then seemed depraved. Perhaps by depravity he actually meant tenderness.

手紙

CHAPTER FOUR / LETTERS

I couldn't make up my mind whether to write to him or what to do. Then, this morning the words of Jesus—"wise as serpents and harmless as doves"—flashed into my head and in a sudden burst of courage I decided to write him a letter.

I am Naoji's sister. If you have forgotten me, please try to remember.

I must apologize that Naoji has again been such a nuisance and caused you such bother. (As a matter of fact, I cannot help feeling that Naoji's affairs are for Naoji to decide, and it is nonsensical for me to offer an apology.) Today I am writing to ask you a favor not for Naoji but for myself. I heard from Naoji that your old place was destroyed during the war and that you have since moved to your present address. I had thought of paying a visit to your house (which seems to be very far out in the suburbs from Tokyo), but of late my mother's health has been rather poor, and I can't possibly leave her to go up to Tokyo. That is why I made up my mind to write you a letter.

There is something I would like to discuss with you.

The matter I have to discuss may appear extremely dubious from the point of view of the usual "Etiquette for Young Women," or even a positive crime, but I—no, we—cannot go on living as we have. I must therefore ask you, the person whom my brother Naoji respects most in the whole world, to be so kind as to listen to my plain, unadorned feelings and to give me the benefit of your guidance.

My present life is unendurable. It is not a matter of like or dislike—we (my mother, Naoji, and myself)—cannot possibly go on living this way.

Yesterday I was in pain and feverish. I was hardly able to breathe and felt at a complete loss what to do with myself. A little after lunch the girl from the farmer's house down the road came in the rain with a load of rice on her back. I handed over to her the clothes I had promised. The girl sat facing me in the dining-room, and as she drank some tea she said, in a really down-to-earth tone, "How much longer can you go on by selling your things?"

"Six months. Perhaps a year," I answered. Then, half covering my face with my right hand, I murmured, "I'm sleepy. I'm so terribly sleepy."

"You're exhausted. It's nervous exhaustion."

"You may be right." At this moment, as I stood on the verge of tears, the words "realism" and "romanticism" welled up within me. I have no sense of realism. And that this very fact might be what permits me to go on living sends cold chills through my whole body. Mother is half an invalid and spends as much time in bed as up. Naoji, as you know, is mentally very sick. While he is here he spends most of his time at the local drinking place, and once every couple of days he takes whatever money we have from selling our clothes and goes off to Tokyo. But that is not what hurts me. I am afraid because I can so clearly foresee my own life rotting away of itself, like a leaf that rots without falling, while I pursue my round of existence from day to day. That is what I find impossible to bear, and why I must escape from my present life, even if it means violating the whole code of young ladies' etiquette. And now I am asking your advice.

I want now to make an open declaration to my mother and to Naoji. I want to state with absolute clarity that I have been in love for some time with a certain man, and that I intend in the future to live as his mistress. I am quite sure you know who it is. His initials are M.C. Whenever anything painful comes up, I am seized with the desire to rush to his house and die of love with him.

M.C. like yourself has a wife and child. He also seems to have women friends more beautiful and younger than I. But I feel that I cannot go on living except by going to him. I have never met M.C.'s wife, but I hear that she is a very sweet and good person. Whenever I think of her, I seem in my own eyes a dreadful woman. I feel, though, that my present life is even more dreadful, and no consideration can make me refrain from appealing to M.C. I would like to fulfill my love "wise as the serpent and harmless as the dove," but I am sure that no one, not my mother or Naoji or the rest of the world, will approve of me. I wonder about you. In short, I have no choice but to think things out myself and act however it seems best to me. The thought brings tears. This is the first thing I have ever had, and I wonder if there is a way to carry it through to the congratulations of those around me. I have strained my mental powers as if I were trying to think of the answer to some terribly complicated problem in algebra, until at last I have come to feel that there is a single point where the whole thing may be unraveled, and suddenly I have become cheerful.

But what does my precious M.C. think of me? That's a disheartening question. You might call me a self-styled—what shall I say, I can't say self-styled wife—perhaps a "self-styled lover." With that the situation, if M.C. says he really can't endure me, I have nothing more to say. I have a favor to ask of you. Could you please ask him? One day six years ago a faint pale rainbow formed in my breast. It was not love or passion, but the colors of the rainbow have deepened and intensified as time has gone by. Never once have I lost it from sight. The rainbow that spans the sky when it clears after a shower soon fades away, but the rainbow in a person's heart does not seem to disappear that way. Please ask him. I wonder what he really thinks of me. I wonder if he has thought of me as of a rainbow in the sky after a shower. And has it already faded away?

If it has, I must erase my own rainbow. But unless I first erase my life, the rainbow in my breast will not fade away.

I pray for an answer.

To Mr. Uehara Jirō. (My Chekhov. M.C.)

P.S. I have recently been putting on a little weight. I think it is less that I am turning into a brute creature than that I have at last become human. This summer I read a novel (just one) by D. H. Lawrence.

No answer has come from you, and I am writing again. The letter I sent the other day was underhanded and full of snares. I suppose that you saw through every one of them. Yes, it's true. I tried to insert a maximum of cunning into every line of the letter. I imagine that you thought that my purpose was merely to elicit money from you to save my life. I don't deny this. However, I would like you to know, if you'll excuse me for saying so, that if my only wish was for a patron I should not have chosen you especially. I have the impression that quite a few rich old men would be willing to care for me. As a matter of fact, not long ago I had something like a proposal. You may even know the gentleman's name—he is a widower over sixty, a member of the Academy of Arts, I believe; this great artist came here to the mountains in order to ask my hand. He used to be a neighbor of ours when we lived in Nishikata Street, and we met him occasionally at neighborhood meetings. Once, it was an evening in autumn as I recall, when Mother and I passed in our car in front of this artist's house, he was standing absent-mindedly by his gate. Mother nodded slightly to him from the car window, at which his peevish, sallow face suddenly turned a brilliant red.

"I wonder if it can be love," I said playfully. "He's in love with you, Mother!"

"No," Mother calmly answered, as if to herself. "He's a great man."

It seems to be our family's custom to honor artists.

The artist sent a proposal for my hand to Mother, by way of a certain prince, one of Uncle Wada's cronies, explaining that he had lost his wife some years ago. Mother suggested that I make a direct reply to the artist in whatever way I saw fit. Without giving it very much thought, I dashed off a note to the effect that I had at present no intention of remarrying.

"You don't mind if I refuse?" I asked Mother.

"I didn't myself think it was a likely match."

I sent my letter of refusal to the artist at his villa in the Japan Alps. Two days later he turned up without warning, having no knowledge of my answer because he had left before my letter reached him. He sent word that he was on his way to a hot spring in Izu and asked to pay a brief call. Artists, whatever their age, seem to indulge in the most childish, irresponsible pranks.

Mother was not feeling well, and I myself received him in the Chinese room. I said while pouring tea, "I imagine that my letter of refusal must have reached your house by now. I carefully considered your offer, but it somehow didn't seem possible."

"Indeed?" he said with some impatience. He wiped away the perspiration. "I hope that you will reconsider. Perhaps I can't—how shall I say it—give you what might be called spiritual happiness, but I can on the other hand make you very happy in a material way. That at least I can assure you. I hope I don't speak too bluntly. . . ."

"I don't understand that happiness you speak of. It may seem very impertinent, but I can only answer, 'No, thank you.' I am what Nietzche described as 'a woman who wants to give birth to a child.' I want a child. Happiness does not interest me. I do want money too, but just enough to be able to bring up my child."

The artist gave an odd smile. "You are a very unusual woman. You can put into words what everyone has thought. To live with you might cause fresh inspiration to come into my work."

He said this rather affected thing in a manner quite unlike an old man. The thought occurred to me that if through my strength the work of so great an artist could really be rejuvenated, this too would certainly be a reason to go on living. But no stretch of the imagination enabled me to visualize myself in the artist's arms.

I asked with a little smile, "Doesn't it make any difference to you that I don't love you?"

He answered seriously, "It doesn't matter for a woman. A woman can be vague."

"But a woman like myself cannot think of marriage without love. I am fully grown. Next year I will be thirty." I was taken aback at my own words.

Thirty. "Something of the maiden's fragrance lingers with a woman until she is twenty-nine, but nothing is left about the body of the woman of thirty years." At the sudden recollection of these words from a French novel I had read long ago, I was assailed by a melancholy I could not drive away. I looked outside. The sea, bathed in the noon glare, glittered with the dazzling intensity of bits of broken glass. I remembered that when I had read those words in the novel, I had lightly assented, thinking them probably true. I felt a sharp nostalgia for those days when I could think with equanimity that a woman's life was over at thirty. I wondered if the maiden fragrance of my body was fading away with each bracelet, necklace, and dress that I sold. A wretched, middle-aged woman. And yet, even a middle-aged woman's life contains a woman's life, doesn't it? That is what I have come of late to understand. I remember what my teacher, an Englishwoman, said to me, then aged nineteen, when she was about to return to her country.

"You should never fall in love. Love will bring

you unhappiness. If you must love, let it be when you are older, after you are thirty."

Her words could only arouse in me a dumb incredulity. It was quite impossible for me at the time even to imagine life after thirty.

The artist suddenly spoke, his voice edged with spite, "I've heard a rumor that you are selling the house. I wonder if it's true."

I laughed. "Excuse me, but I just remembered The Cherry Orchard. I suppose you would like to buy it?"

He twisted his mouth in an angry scowl and did not answer. Artist that he was, he was quick to guess my meaning.

It was true that there had been talk of selling the house to a prince, but it had never come to anything, and I was surprised that the artist had even heard the rumor. But that we should have been thinking of him in terms of Lopákhin in The Cherry Orchard was so distasteful that he quite lost his good humor, and after a few minutes more of small talk, he left.

What I ask of you now is not that you be a Lopákhin. That much I can warrant you. But please listen to the presumption of a middle-aged woman.

It is already six years since we met. At the time I knew nothing about you except that you were my brother's teacher, and at that a rather peculiar teacher. We drank saké together from glasses, and *you were a little bold. That didn't bother me. It only gave me the most curious sensation of buoyancy. I didn't like or dislike you—I had no feeling at all. Later, in order to please my brother, I borrowed some of your novels from him and read them. Sometimes I found them interesting, sometimes not. I confess I was not a very passionate reader. But during the past six years, from just when I can't say, the remembrance of you has soaked into me like some all-pervasive fog, and what we did that night on the stairs from the basement has returned to me with absolute vividness. I feel somehow as if that moment was vital enough to decide my fate. I miss you. Perhaps, I think, it may be love, and at this possibility I have felt so utterly forlorn that I have sometimes yielded to uncontrolled weeping. You are completely unlike other men. I am not in love with an author, like Nina in* The Sea Gull. *I am not fascinated by novelists. If you think me a "literary lady" or anything of the kind, you are off the track. I want a child from you.*

Perhaps if I had met you long, long ago, when you and I were both still single, we might have married, and I should have been spared my present sufferings, but I have resigned myself to the fact that I shall never be able to marry you. For me to attempt to push aside your wife would be like an act of brute force, and I should hate myself for it. I am willing to become your mistress. (I really can't bear the word, but when I was on the point of writing "lover," I realized that I meant what people generally do by the word "mistress," and I decided to be blunt.) I gather that the usual mistress has a hard lot. They say that she is abandoned as soon as she ceases to be of use, and that a man, whatever sort of man he may be, will always return to his wife when he approaches sixty. I remember hearing my nurse and the old man of Nishikata Street discussing this matter and concluding that a mistress was one thing a woman should never become. But they were talking about an ordinary mistress, and I feel that our case is different.

I believe that your work is the most precious thing in the world to you, and that if you like me, becoming intimate with me may actually help your work. And your wife would then also be willing to accept our relationship. I know this may seem an odd kind of sophistry, but I am convinced that there is nothing amiss with my reasoning.

The only problem is your answer. Do you like me or dislike me? Or have you no feelings on the subject? I am terrified at what you may reply, but I must ask anyway. In my last letter, I wrote that I was a "self-styled lover," and in this letter, I have written about the "presumption of a middle-aged woman." It now occurs to me that unless you answer I shall have no grounds whatsoever even for presumption and shall probably be doomed to waste away the rest of my life alone. I am lost unless I hear from you.

In your novels you often describe love adventures, and people gossip about you as if you were an absolute monster, but it has suddenly dawned on me that you probably are actually an advocate of common sense. I do not myself understand common sense. I believe that the good life consists in being able to do what I like. I want to give birth to your child. I don't want to bear anyone else's child, no matter what happens. I ask your advice. If you know the answer, please tell me. Please say clearly what your feelings are.

The rain has stopped and a wind has sprung up. It is now three o'clock in the afternoon. I shall go out now to get our ration of the best quality saké. I shall put two empty rum bottles in a bag and this letter in my pocket, and in ten minutes I shall be on my way to the village down the hill. I shall not let my brother get this saké. I myself intend to drink it. Every night I drink a little from a glass. You know, saké really should be drunk from a glass.

Won't you come here?

To Mr. M.C.

It rained again today. An invisible, nasty mixture of fog and rain is falling. Every day I have waited for your answer without even leaving the house, but nothing has come. What are you thinking about? I wonder if I did the wrong thing in my last letter in writing about that artist. Perhaps you thought I mentioned his proposal in order to arouse your competitive spirit. But nothing more has come of it. Just a little while ago, as a matter of fact, Mother and I were laughing over it. Mother has recently been complaining about pain in her tongue, but thanks to the "aesthetic treatment" which Naoji prescribed, the pain has been much alleviated, and she has seemed rather better of late.

A few minutes ago I was standing on the porch, and as I looked at the rain being blown and swirled about, I was trying to picture what your feelings are. Just then Mother's voice called from the dining-room, "I have finished boiling the milk. Please come here."

"It's so cold today I've made the milk very hot," she said.

As we drank the steaming milk, we talked about the artist. I said, "He and I are not the least suited, are we?"

Mother answered tranquilly, "No, you aren't."

"Considering the wayward type I am, that I don't dislike artists and, what's more, that he seems to have a large income, it certainly looked like a good match. But it's quite impossible."

Mother smiled. "Kazuko, you're a naughty child.

If you were so sure that it was impossible, why in the world did you lead him on that way by chattering with such relish when he was here? I can't imagine your motive."

"Oh, but it was interesting. There's a lot more I would like to have talked about. I have no discretion, you know."

"No, you never let anybody go in a conversation. Kazuko, you're tenacious!"

Mother was in very good spirits today. Then, noticing that I had put my hair up yesterday for the first time, she commented, "That style is made for women with thin hair. Your up-sweep looks much too grand. All that is missing is a little golden tiara. I'm afraid it's a failure."

"I'm disappointed. Didn't you once tell me that my neckline was so pretty that I should try not to hide it? Didn't you?"

"Yes, I seem to remember something of the sort."

"I never forget a syllable of praise addressed to me. I'm so glad you remembered."

"That gentleman who came the other day must have praised you."

"Yes, he did. That's why I wouldn't let him out of my clutches. He said that being with me made his inspiration—no, I can't go on. It isn't that I dislike artists, but I can't stand anyone who puts on those ponderous airs of a man of character."

"What kind of man is Naoji's teacher?"

I felt a chill go through me. "I don't really know, but what can you expect from a teacher of Naoji's. He seems to be tagged as a dissolute character."

"Tagged?" murmured Mother with a pleased look in her eyes. "That's an interesting expression. If he wears a tag, doesn't that make him harmless? It sounds rather sweet, like a kitten with a bell around its neck. A dissolute character without a tag is what frightens me."

"I wonder."

I felt happy, so happy; it was as though my body had dissolved into smoke and was being drawn up into the sky. Do you understand? Why I was so happy? If you don't, I'll hit you!

Won't you come here sometime? I would ask Naoji to bring you back with him, but there's something unnatural and peculiar about asking him. It would be best if you suddenly dropped in, as if acting on some whim of yours. It wouldn't matter much if you came with Naoji, but still, it would be best if it were by yourself, when Naoji is away in Tokyo. If Naoji is here, he is sure to monopolize you, and you will be taken off to Osaki's place to drink, and that will be that.

My family for generations has always been fond of artists. Kōrin himself lived for years in our old family house in Kyoto and painted beautiful pictures there. So I am sure Mother will be very pleased to have you come. You will probably stay in the foreign-style room on the second floor. Please do not forget to turn off the light. I will climb the dark stairs with a little candle in my hand. You don't approve? Too fast, I suppose!

I like dissolute people, especially those who wear their tags. I would like to become dissolute myself. I feel as if there is no other way for me to live. You are the most notorious example in Japan of a tagged dissolute, I suppose. Naoji has told me that many people say you are dirty and repulsive, and that you are hated and often attacked. Such stories only make me love you all the more. I am sure, considering who you are, that you must have all kinds of amies, *but now you will gradually come to love only me. I can't help thinking that. When you are living with me, you will be happy in your work. Ever since I was small, people have often told me that to be with me is to forget one's troubles. I have never had the experience of being disliked. Everyone has called me a "nice girl." That's why I am so sure that you could never dislike me.*

It would be so good if we could meet. I no longer need an answer from you or anything else. I want to meet you. I suppose that the simplest thing would be for me to go to your house in Tokyo, but I am Mother's nurse and servant in constant attendance, and I couldn't possibly leave her. I beg you. Please come here. I want to meet you just once. Then you will understand everything. See the faint lines that have etched themselves on both sides of my mouth. Behold the wrinkles of the malheur du siècle. *I am sure that my face will express my feeling to you more clearly than any words.*

In my first letter I wrote of a rainbow in my breast. That rainbow is not of the refined beauty of the light of fireflies or of the stars. If it were so faint and faraway, I would not be suffering this way, and I could probably forget you gradually. The rainbow in my breast is a bridge of flames. It is a sensation so strong that it chars my breast. Not even the craving of a narcotics addict when his drugs run out can be as painful as this. I am certain that I am not mistaken, that it is not wicked of me, but even when most persuaded, I sometimes shudder at the thought that I may be attempting to do an extraordinarily foolish thing. And I often wonder if I am not going mad. However, sometimes even I am capable of making plans with due self-possession. Please come here just this once. Any time at all will suit me. I will wait here for you and not go anywhere. Please believe me.

Please see me again and then, if you dislike me, say so plainly. The flames in my breast were lighted by you; it is up to you to extinguish them. I can't put them out by my unaided efforts. If we meet, if we can only meet, I know that I shall be saved. Were these the days of The Tale of Genji, *what I am saying now would not be anything exceptional, but today—oh, my ambition is to become your mistress and the mother of your child.*

If there is anyone who would laugh at letters like these, he is a man who derides a woman's efforts to go on living, he mocks at a woman's life. I am choking in the suffocating foul air of the harbor. I want to hoist my sails in the open sea, even though a tempest may be blowing. Furled sails are always dirty. Those who would deride me are so many furled sails. They can do nothing.

A nuisance of a woman. But in this matter, it is I who suffer the most. It is nonsensical for some outsider who has never suffered the least of what I have been going through to presume to make judgments while slackly drooping his ugly sails. I have no desire for others to take it on themselves to analyze my thoughts. I am without thoughts. I have never, not even once, acted on the basis of any doctrine or philosophy.

I am convinced that those people whom the world considers good and respects are all liars and fakes. I do not trust the world. My only ally is the tagged dissolute. The tagged dissolute. That is the only cross on which I wish to be crucified. Though ten thousand people criticize me, I can throw in their teeth my challenge: Are you not all the more dangerous for being without tags?

Do you understand?

There is no reason in love, and I have gone rather too far in offering you these rational-seeming arguments. I feel as if I am merely parroting my brother. All I want to say is that I await your visit. I want to see you again. That is all.

To wait. In our lives we know joy, anger, sorrow, and a hundred other emotions, but these emotions all together occupy a bare one per cent of our time. The remaining ninety-nine per cent is just living in waiting. I wait in momentary expectation, feeling as though my breasts are being crushed, for the sound in the corridor of the footsteps of happiness. Empty. Oh, life is too painful, the reality that confirms the universal belief that it is best not to be born.

Thus every day, from morning to night, I wait in despair for something. I wish I could be glad that I was born, that I am alive, that there are people and a world.

Won't you shove aside the morality that blocks you?

To M.C. (These are not the initials of My Chekhov. I am not in love with an author. My Child.)

CHAPTER FIVE / THE LADY

This summer I sent three letters to him. But no reply came. It seemed at the time that there was nothing else I could possibly do, and I put into the three letters all that was in my heart. I posted them with the feeling of one who leaps from a promontory into the raging billows of the sea, but although I waited a very long time, no answer came.

I casually inquired of my brother Naoji how that man was. Naoji replied that he was much the same as usual—that he spent every night in drunken carousals, that his literary productions consisted exclusively of works of an increasingly immoral nature, and that he was the object of the scorn and loathing of all decent citizens. Moreover, he had urged Naoji to start a publishing house, a suggestion which Naoji eagerly accepted. As a preliminary step, Naoji persuaded two or three novelists besides that person to appoint him as their agent, and the question now was whether or not they could unearth someone with capital to lend the project. As I listened to Naoji's words, it became increasingly evident that not a particle of my odor had seeped into the atmosphere around the man I loved. It was not so much shame that I experienced as the feeling that the actual world was an unfamiliar organism utterly unlike the world of my imagination. I was assailed by a sensation of desolation more intense than anything I had previously known, as if I had been abandoned at dusk in an autumnal wasteland where no answering sound would ever come, however often I called. Is that, I wonder, what is meant by the pat phrase "disappointed love"? I asked myself if I were doomed to die, numbed by the night dews, alone in the wasteland as the sun dropped completely from sight. My shoulders and chest were fiercely shaken, and I was choked by a dry sobbing.

There is nothing left for me now but to go up to

Tokyo, cost what it may, and see Mr. Uehara. My sails have been lifted, and my ship has put forth from the harbor. I can not wait any longer. I must go where I am going. These were my thoughts as I began secretly to prepare for the journey to Tokyo, only to have Mother's condition take an unexpected turn.

One night she was racked by a terrible cough. When I took her temperature, it was already 102 degrees.

"It must be because it was so chilly today," Mother murmured in between spasms of coughing. "Tomorrow I'll be better." But somehow it didn't seem just a cough, and to be on the safe side I decided to have the village doctor pay a call the following day.

The next morning Mother's temperature dropped to normal and her cough had much abated. All the same, I went to the doctor and asked him to examine Mother, describing her sudden weakening of late, her fever of the previous night, and my belief that there was more to her cough than a mere cold.

"I shall be calling presently," the doctor said, adding, "and here is a gift for you." He took three pears from a shelf in the corner of his reception room and offered them to me. He appeared a little after noon in his formal clothes. As usual he spent an interminable time in ausculation and percussion, at last turning to me with the words, "There is nothing to excite alarm. If your mother takes the medicine which I shall prescribe, she will recover."

I found him curiously comic but controlled my smiles to ask, "How about injections?"

He answered gravely, "They will probably not be necessary. We have here to do with a cold, and if your mother remains quiet, I think we can get rid of it shortly."

But even after a week had passed Mother's temperature did not disappear. Her cough was better, but her temperature fluctuated between 99 in the morning and 102 degrees at night. Just at this juncture the doctor took to bed with an upset stomach. I went to his house for some medicine and took the occasion to describe Mother's discouraging condition to the nurse, who transmitted my words to the doctor. "It's an ordinary cold and should cause no anxiety," was his reply. I was given a liquid medicine and a powder.

Naoji as usual was off in Tōkyo. It had already been more than ten days since he left. Alone and in an excess of depression, I wrote a postcard to my Uncle Wada informing him of the change in Mother's health.

Some days later the village doctor called with the news that his stomach indisposition had at length passed.

He examined Mother's chest with an expression

of rapt concentration. Suddenly he cried, "Ah, I know what it is! I know what it is!" Again turning toward me, he intoned, "I have understood the cause of the fever. A seepage has developed in the left lung. Nevertheless, there is no need for anxiety. The fever will probably continue for the time being, but if your mother remains quiet, there is no cause for alarm."

"I wonder," I thought, but like a drowning man clutching at a straw, I took whatever comfort I could from his diagnosis.

After the doctor had made his departure, I exclaimed, "Isn't that a relief, Mother? Just a little seepage—why, most people have *that*. As long as you can just keep your spirits up, you'll be better in no time. The weather this summer has been so unseasonal. That's where the trouble lies. I hate the summer. I hate summer flowers too."

Mother, her eyes shut, smiled. "They say that people who like summer flowers die in the summer, and I was expecting to die this summer, perhaps, but now that Naoji has come home I have held on until autumn."

It was painful for me to realize that Naoji, even such as he was, had become the mainstay of Mother's pleasure in life.

"Well, then, since summer has passed, that means we're over the hump of your danger period, doesn't it? Mother, the bush clover is in bloom in the garden.

And valerian, burnet, bellflowers, timothy—the whole garden reeks of autumn. I am sure that once it's October your temperature will go down."

I am praying that it will. What a relief it will be when the sticky, lingering September heat has passed! Then, when the chrysanthemums are in bloom and one day of bright Indian summer succeeds another, Mother's fever will surely disappear. She will grow strong, and I will be able to see him. Perhaps my plans will come to magnificent flowering like some gigantic chrysanthemum. Oh, if only it were already October, and Mother's fever were gone!

About a week after I wrote my uncle, he arranged for an old doctor named Miyake, who had once served as a court physician, to come from Tokyo to examine Mother.

Dr. Miyake had been an acquaintance of my father's, and Mother looked delighted to see him. His rough manners and coarse speech, for which he had long been famous, also apparently endeared him to Mother. They had not got around to a formal examination, and the two of them were diverting themselves instead with an uninihibited bout of gossip. I went to the kitchen to make some pudding, and by the time it was ready to be served the examination had already been concluded. The doctor, his ausculator dangling from his shoulders like a necklace, slouched in a wicker chair.

"Fellows like myself go into some roadside joint to take a stand-up lunch of noodles. You never get anything good or—for that matter—really bad," he was saying as I entered, and this, I suppose, was typical of their conversation. Mother was following his words with an unconstrained expression.

"It wasn't anything after all!" I exclaimed to myself with a sigh of relief. Suddenly courage welled up in me and I asked, "How is she? The village doctor said there was a seepage in her left lung. Do you think so too?"

The doctor replied offhandedly, "What's all that? She's perfectly all right!"

"Oh, I'm so relieved, aren't you, Mother?" I spoke to her, smiling from my heart. "He says you're all right."

Dr. Miyake at this point rose from his chair and walked into the Chinese room. He obviously had something to disclose to me. I tiptoed out of the room behind him.

He stopped when he reached the wall hanging and said, "I hear a funny sound."

"It isn't a seepage?"

"No."

"Bronchitis?" I was already in tears as I asked.

"No."

T.B. I didn't want to think of it. I was sure that with my strength I could cure pneumonia or a seepage or bronchitis. But tuberculosis—perhaps it was already too late. I felt as if my legs were crumbling under me.

"Is the sound very bad, that funny sound you hear?" I was sobbing helplessly.

"Right and left both—the whole works!"

"But Mother's still healthy! She enjoys her meals so!"

"It can't be helped."

"That's not true. It can't be. If she eats lots of butter, eggs, and milk, she'll recover, won't she? As long as she keeps up her resistance, the fever will go down, won't it?"

"She should eat a lot of whatever she likes."

"Isn't that what I said? Every day she eats five tomatoes alone."

"Tomatoes are good."

"Then it's all right? She'll get better?"

"This sickness may prove fatal. It's best that you should know it."

This was the first time in my life that I had become aware of the existence of the wall of despair built of all the many things in the world before which human strength is helpless.

"Two years? Three years?" I whispered, trembling.

"I can't say. In any case, nothing can be done about it."

Dr. Miyake departed, mumbling something about reservations for that day at Nagaoka Hot Spring. I saw him as far as the gate. Dazedly I walked back to Mother's bed. I forced a smile, as much as to say that nothing was wrong, but Mother asked, "What did the doctor tell you?"

"He says that everything will be all right if your temperature only goes down."

"What about my chest?"

"Apparently it's nothing serious. It's like when you were sick before. I'm sure of that. Just as soon as the weather turns a bit cooler, you'll quickly get back your strength."

I tried to believe my own lies. I tried to forget the terrifying word "fatal." I couldn't believe it was the truth. I had the feeling that were Mother to die, my own flesh would melt away with her. From now on, I thought, I will forget everything else except preparing all kinds of delicious things for Mother. Fish, soup, liver, broth, tomatoes, eggs, milk, salad—I will sell everything I own to buy food for Mother.

I went to the Chinese room and dragged the reclining chair out to a spot on the veranda from where I could see Mother. She did not look the least like a sick person. Her eyes were beautifully clear and her complexion fresh. Her fever only comes in the afternoon.

"How well Mother looks!" I thought. "I am sure

she must be all right." In my heart I had blotted out Dr. Miyake's diagnosis.

My mind faded off into a reverie on how much better it would be when it was October and the chrysanthemums were in bloom. Before I knew it I had dozed off and was standing in a landscape which occasionally comes to me in dreams, although I have never actually seen it. I was beside a lake in the forest so long familiar to me, and the sight of that landscape came with a thrill of recognition. I was walking next to a boy in Japanese clothes, silently, with no sound of footsteps. The whole landscape seemed veiled in a kind of green fog. A delicate white bridge lay submerged at the bottom of the lake.

The boy spoke. "The bridge has sunk! We can't go anywhere today. Let's stop at the hotel here. I'm sure there must be an empty room."

There was a hotel on the edge of the lake. Its stone walls dripped with the green fog. On a stone gate the words "Hotel Switzerland" were carved in gilt letters. As I read the letters SWI, I suddenly thought of Mother. I wondered uneasily how she was, whether she, too, were staying at this hotel. I passed with the young man through the gate into the front garden. Huge red flowers like hydrangeas were blooming with a burning intensity in the foggy garden. When I was a child, the bedcovers had a pattern of crimson hydrangeas which had always made me feel peculiarly unhappy. But, I thought now, there really are such things as red hydrangeas.

"You aren't cold?"

"No. Just a little. My ears are wet with the fog, and the insides are cold." I laughed and asked him, "I wonder what has happened to Mother?"

The boy answered with a smile at once heartbreakingly sad and full of compassion, "She is in her grave."

A cry escaped my lips. That was it. Mother was no longer with us. And hadn't a funeral already taken place? At this realization of Mother's death, my body shook with an indescribable loneliness and my eyes opened.

It was already dusk on the veranda. It was raining. A green-colored desolation lingered over everything, just as in the dream.

"Mother?" I called.

She answered in a calm voice. "What are you doing there?"

I leaped up with joy and rushed to her side. "I was sleeping."

"I wondered what you were doing. That was a long nap, wasn't it?" She seemed amused with me.

I was so overjoyed at Mother's charm, at her being alive, that my eyes filled with tears of gratitude.

"And what are my lady's commands for dinner this evening?" I asked rather archly.

"Please don't bother. I don't need anything. Today my temperature went up to 103 degrees."

From happiness I was suddenly plunged into blank despair. At a loss what to do, I let my glance wander vacantly around the dimly lit room. I wanted to die.

"Why should that be, I wonder. 103 degrees!"

"It's nothing. It is only just the moments before the fever breaks out that I don't like. My head hurts a little, I feel a chill, and then the fever comes."

Outside it was dark now. The rain had stopped, but a wind was blowing. I switched on the lights and was about to go to the dining-room when Mother called out, "The light hurts my eyes. Please leave it off."

"But you won't like lying in the dark that way, will you?" I asked, still hesitating by the switch.

"It doesn't matter. When I sleep my eyes are shut. I don't feel the least bit lonely in the dark. It's the glare that I dislike so. Let's not put the lights on in this room from now on."

Her words filled me with foreboding. Without a word I switched out the lights in Mother's room. I turned on a lamp in the next room and, feeling unbearably depressed, hurried to the kitchen. As I sat there, eating canned salmon and cold rice, heavy tears fell from my eyes.

With nightfall the wind began to blow harder

and developed by about nine into a real gale with pelting rain. The porch blinds, which I had rolled up a couple of days earlier, clattered in the wind. I sat in the room next to Mother's, reading with a strange agitation Rosa Luxemburg's *Introduction to Economics.* I had borrowed this book from Naoji's room (without his permission, naturally) along with the *Selected Works of Lenin* and Kautsky's *Social Revolution.* I had left them on my desk. One morning, when Mother passed beside my desk on her way to the bath, she happened to notice the three volumes. She picked them up one after another, examined the contents, and then, with a little sigh, returned them softly to the desk. She glanced at me sorrowfully as she did so. A profound grief filled her look, but it was by no means one of rejection or antipathy. Mother's chosen reading matter is Hugo, Dumas *père et fils,* Musset, and Daudet, but I know that even such books of sweet romances are permeated with the smell of revolution.

People like Mother who possess a Heaven-given education—the words are peculiar I know—may perhaps be able to welcome a revolution in a surprisingly matter-of-fact way, as a quite natural occurrence. Even I found some things rather objectionable when I read Rosa Luxemburg's book, but, given the sort of person I am, the experience on the whole was one of profound interest. The subject matter of her book is generally considered to be economics, but if it is read as economics, it is boring beyond belief. It contains nothing but exceedingly obvious platitudes. It may be, of course, that I have no understanding of economics. Be that as it may, the subject holds not the slightest interest for me. A science which is postulated on the assumption that human beings are avaricious and will remain avaricious through all eternity is utterly devoid of point (whether in problems of distribution or any other aspect) to a person who is not avaricious. And yet as I read this book, I felt a strange excitement for quite another reason—the sheer courage the author demonstrated in tearing apart without any hesitation all manner of conventional ideas. However much I may oppose morality, I am powerless to prevent the image floating before my eyes of the wife of the man I love, coolly and quickly hurrying back to his house. Then my thoughts turn destructive. Destruction is tragic and piteous and beautiful. The dream of destroying, building anew, perfecting. Perhaps even, once one has destroyed, the day of perfecting may never come, but in the passion of love I must destroy. I must start a revolution. Rosa gave tragically her undivided love to Marxism.

It was a winter twelve years ago.

"You're just like that spineless girl in the *Sara-*

shina Diary who never can open her mouth. It's impossible to talk to you."

My friend, so saying, walked away. I had just returned her, unread, a book by Lenin.

"Have you read it?"

"I'm sorry. I haven't."

It was on a bridge from which you could see the Tokyo Russian Orthodox Cathedral.

"Why? What was the trouble?"

My friend was about an inch taller than I and very gifted in languages. Her red beret became her. She was a beautiful girl with a face which was reputed to look like the Mona Lisa's.

"I hated the color of the jacket."

"You *are* strange. That wasn't the real reason, I'm sure. Wasn't it because you've become afraid of me?"

"I am not afraid of you. I couldn't stand the color of the jacket."

"I see." She spoke sadly. It was then that she compared me to the girl in the *Sarashina Diary* and decided that it was no use talking to me.

We stood for a while in silence looking down at the wintry river.

" 'Farewell, if this should be our parting forever, forever farewell.' Byron." She murmured and then quickly recited the verses of Byron in the original English. She gave me a light embrace.

I felt ashamed of myself and whispered an

apology. I began to walk toward the station. I looked back once over my shoulder and saw my friend still standing motionless on the bridge, staring at me.

That was the last time I saw her. We used to go to the same foreign teacher's house, but we were in a different school.

Twelve years have passed and I have yet to progress a step beyond the *Sarashina Diary* stage. What in the world have I been doing all this time? I have never felt myself drawn toward revolution, and I have not even known love. The older and wiser heads of the world have always described revolution and love to us as the two most foolish and loathsome of human activities. Before the war, even during the war, we were convinced of it. Since the defeat, however, we no longer trust the older and wiser heads and have come to feel that the opposite of whatever they say is the real truth about life. Revolution and love are in fact the best, most pleasurable things in the world, and we realize it is precisely because they are so good that the older and wiser heads have spitefully fobbed off on us their sour grapes of a lie. This I want to believe implicitly: Man was born for love and revolution.

The door slid open suddenly and Mother poked in her smiling face. "You're still up. Aren't you sleepy?"

I looked at the clock on my desk. It was midnight.

"No, I'm not the least bit sleepy. I have been reading a book about Socialism and I'm all worked up over it."

"Oh. Haven't we anything to drink in the house? The best thing when you're in such a state is to have a drink before you go to bed. Then you'll be able to sleep soundly." She spoke in a bantering tone, but there was an indefinable something in her attitude, a coquetry just a hair's breadth removed from dissoluteness.

October came at last, but it didn't bring any sudden change to bright autumn weather. Instead, one hot, humid day followed another, rather as it does during the rainy season. And every evening Mother's fever hovered a little over a hundred.

One morning I noticed something frightening. Mother's hand was swollen. This was just about the time when Mother, who had always enjoyed breakfast most of any meal, would only sit up in bed to eat a little rice gruel. She could not swallow anything with a strong odor. On that day she seemed to find distasteful even the smell of the mushrooms in the soup I had made. She lifted the bowl to her lips but returned it untouched to the tray. It was then that I noticed to my astonishment that Mother's right hand was swollen.

"Mother! What's happened to your hand?"

Her face also seemed rather pale and puffy. "It isn't anything. This much of a swelling doesn't mean anything."

"How long has it been that way?"

Mother remained silent, a dazed expression on her face. I wanted to weep aloud. That distorted hand did not belong to my mother. It was some other woman's hand. Mother's hand is smaller and more delicate. A hand I know well. A gentle hand. A lovable hand. Had that hand, I wondered, vanished forever? The left hand as yet was not so swollen. But it was too painful for me to go on looking at Mother. I turned away my eyes and glared at a basket of flowers in a corner of the room.

I felt the tears coming. Unable to bear more, I got up abruptly and fled to the kitchen. There I found Naoji eating a soft-boiled egg. On the rare occasions when he was at home, he was certain to spend the night carousing at Osaki's place. The morning after I would find him in the kitchen morosely eating soft-boiled eggs, the only nourishment he would take. Then he would make his way back to the second floor, where he would spend his day in and out of bed.

"Mother's hand is swollen," I said, my eyes on the floor. I couldn't go on. I was weeping convulsively.

Naoji did not reply.

I lifted my head. "It's hopeless now. Haven't you noticed? When there's a swelling like that, there's no hope." My hands were clenched on the end of the table.

Naoji's face also took on a gloomy expression. "It won't be long. Damn. What a disgusting thing to happen."

"I want to bring her back to health again. I want somehow to save her," I said, wringing my hands. Suddenly Naoji burst into tears. "Don't you see there's nothing we can do? We can't do a thing." He rubbed his eyes furiously with his fists.

That day Naoji went to Tokyo to inform Uncle Wada of Mother's condition and to get instructions for the future. Almost every minute I was not actually by Mother's side, I spent in weeping. When I went out in the morning fog to fetch the milk, when I smoothed my hair before the mirror, when I put on lipstick, it was always with tears. Happy days I had spent with Mother, this event and that, flashed like pictures before my eyes. There was no limit—and no use—to my tears. That evening when it grew dark I went out on the veranda of the Chinese room and sat sobbing for a long time. The stars were sparkling in the autumn sky, and at my feet a cat, I don't know whose, was curled, motionless.

The next day the swelling in Mother's hand was

even worse. She did not eat anything at mealtimes. She could not even drink orange juice, she said, because her throat was so rough and painful.

"Mother, how would it be if you put on again that mask Naoji recommended?" I had intended to soften my words with a smile, but even as I spoke I broke into a wail of anguish.

Mother said gently, "You must be worn out from the strain every day. Please hire a nurse for me." I realized that she was more worried about my health than her own, and this made me feel all the more miserable.

A little after noon Naoji arrived with Dr. Miyake and a nurse. The old doctor, who normally gave forth nothing but jokes, rushed this time into the sickroom in a kind of rage and at once began his examination. This concluded, he muttered to no one in particular, "She's grown weaker." He gave Mother a camphor injection.

"Have you a place to stay, doctor?" Mother asked in a delirium.

"At Nagaoka again. I have a reservation, so there's nothing for you to worry about. Instead of fretting about other people, you must think more of yourself and eat a great deal of whatever you like, anything and everything. If you take nourishment you'll get better. I'll be back tomorrow. I'm leaving my nurse behind, and please make good use of her." The doctor addressed his words in a loud voice to Mother's sickbed, then gave a signal with his eyes to Naoji. Naoji went by himself to show the doctor to the gate. When he returned a few minutes later the expression on his face betrayed that he was holding back his tears. We tiptoed out of the sickroom and went to the dining-room.

"Is it hopeless? What did he say?"

Naoji twisted his mouth into a smile. "Disgusting. Her weakness seems to have grown much more pronounced. The doctor said that the end might come in a day or two." His eyes filled with tears as he spoke.

"I wonder if we shouldn't send telegrams to everyone," I said. I was surprisingly self-possessed.

"I discussed that with Uncle Wada, but he said that as we are now we can't afford such a big gathering. Even supposing people would come, the house is so small that we couldn't very well ask them to stay here, and there are no decent hotels in the neighborhood. In other words, he says that we are poor now and haven't the means to send for all the *grands seigneurs* in our family. Uncle Wada is supposed to come here immediately, but he's always been such a miser that we can't depend on him to help us. Even last night, of all times, he forgot Mama's illness long enough to give me a severe lecture. Never in all the course of world history has anyone ever seen the light as the result of being preached to by a miser. There's all the difference between him and us, let alone Mama. He makes me sick."

"But after all, I, or at any rate you, will now be dependent on him."

"Nothing doing. I'd rather become a beggar. You, my dear sister, will be the one who will have to depend on his favors."

"I—" the tears came, "I have somewhere to go."

"A marriage? Is it settled?"

"No."

"Self-support? The working woman! Don't make me laugh!"

"No, not self-support. I will become a revolutionary."

"What!" Naoji looked at me with an odd expression.

Just then the nurse called. "Your mother seems to want you for something."

I rushed to the sickroom and sat beside her bed. "What is it?" I asked, bending my head over hers.

Mother remained silent, but I could tell that she wished to say something.

"Water?"

She shook her head faintly. After a while she said in a small voice, "I had a dream."

"What kind of dream?"

"About a snake."

I was startled.

"I believe you'll find a female snake with red stripes on the step in front of the porch. Please go and look."

I stood up with a feeling of growing cold all over. I went to the porch and looked through the glass door. On the step a snake was stretched out full length in the autumn sun. I felt dizzy.

I know who you are. You are a little bigger and older than when I saw you last, but you are the snake whose eggs I burned. I have already felt your vengeance, so go away at once.

This prayer went through my head as I stood there, my eyes riveted on the snake, which gave no indication of stirring. For whatever reason, I didn't want the snake to be seen by the nurse. I stamped my foot. "No," I cried in a voice that was louder than necessary, "there's no snake here, Mother. Your dream was not true." I looked again at the step and saw that the snake had at last moved and was slowly gliding away.

There was no hope, none. Resignation first began to germinate in my heart after I saw the snake. I had heard that when my Father died there was a small black snake by his bed, and I myself had seen a snake twisted around every tree in the garden.

Mother seemed to have lost the strength to sit up in bed and remained in a perpetual doze. I put the nurse completely in charge of her. As for food, it now could barely pass Mother's throat. After seeing the snake the tension in my heart had melted into something akin to a sensation of happiness, peace of mind one might even say, at the realization that I had now reached the very bottom of agony. My only thought now was to be with Mother as much as I could.

I spent the whole of the next day close to Mother's bedside, knitting. I am much faster than most people at knitting or sewing, but not very proficient at it. Mother used always to point out place after place in my knitting that was poorly done. That day I did not feel particularly like knitting, but I took out my box of yarn and for appearance's sake, so that Mother would not think it strange that I spent all my time glued to her bedside, began to knit with a determination that suggested I had no other thought in the world.

Mother stared at my hands. "You're making socks for yourself, aren't you? Don't forget, unless you increase the length by eight they'll be tight when you wear them."

When I was a child I could never knit properly, no matter how much Mother helped me, and now I discovered myself just as upset as I used to get then, only to be swept by nostalgia at the thought that this was the last time that Mother would ever guide me. I could not see my knitting for the tears.

Mother did not appear in any pain as she lay there. She had not taken any food since morning, and all I had done was to moisten her lips occasionally with gauze soaked in tea. However, she was quite conscious and spoke to me from time to time in a composed tone. "I seem to recall having seen a picture of the Emperor in the newspaper. I'd like to look at it again."

I held that section of the newspaper above Mother's face.

"He's grown old."

"No, it's a poor photograph. In the photographs they printed the other day he seemed really young and cheerful. He probably is happier these days than ever."

"Why?"

"The Emperor has been liberated too."

Mother smiled sadly and said, "Even when I want to cry, the tears don't come any more."

I suddenly wondered whether Mother might not actually be happy now, whether the sensation of happiness might not be something like faintly glittering gold sunken at the bottom of the river of sorrow. The feeling of that strange pale light when once one has exceeded all the bounds of unhappiness—if that can be called a sensation of happiness, the Emperor, my mother, and even I myself may be said to be happy now.

A calm autumn morning. A sunlit, mellow autumn garden. I put down my knitting and looked off at the sea sparkling in the distance. "Mother," I said, "I have been very ignorant of the world until now." There was much more I wanted to say, but I was ashamed lest the nurse, who was making preparations in a corner of the room for a vein injection, should hear, and I stopped abruptly.

"You say until now." Mother with a wan smile caught me up on my words. "You mean that now you understand the world?"

Inexplicably, my face crimsoned.

"I don't understand the world." Mother turned her face away. She spoke in a low voice, almost to herself.

"I don't either. I wonder if anyone does. We all remain children, no matter how much time goes by. We don't understand anything."

I must go on living. And, though it may be childish of me, I can't go on in simple compliance. From now on I must struggle with the world. I thought that Mother might well be the last of those who can end their lives beautifully and sadly, struggling with no one, neither hating nor betraying anyone. In the world to come there will be no room for such people. The dying are beautiful, but to live, to survive—those things somehow seem hideous and contaminated with blood. I curled myself on the floor and tried to twist my body into the posture, as I remembered it, of a pregnant snake digging a hole. But there was something to which I could not resign myself. Call it low-minded of me, if you will, I must survive and struggle with the world in order to accomplish my desires. Now that it was clear that Mother would soon die, my romanticism and sentimentality were gradually vanishing, and I felt as though I were turning into a calculating, unprincipled creature.

Shortly after noon, while I sat next to Mother, moistening her lips, an automobile stopped in front of our gate. My uncle Wada and my aunt had arrived from Tokyo. My uncle at once went into the sickroom and sat himself without a word by Mother's bedside. Mother hid the lower part of her face with a handkerchief and, not taking her eyes from my uncle's face, began to weep. But there were no tears. She made me think of a doll.

"Where's Naoji?" Mother asked after a while, looking at me.

I went up to the second floor. Naoji was sprawled on a sofa reading a magazine. "Mother is calling for you," I said.

"What—another tragic scene? O ye of strong nerves and shallow feelings, have patience and do your duty! We who truly suffer—though indeed the spirit is willing, the flesh is weak—we by no means have the energy to sit with Mama." He flung on his jacket and went downstairs with me.

When we had seated ourselves side by side near Mother's pillow, she suddenly thrust her hand out from under the covers and silently pointed first at Naoji and then at me. Turning next to my uncle, she joined her hands together in supplication.

My uncle nodded expansively. "Yes. I understand, I understand."

Mother shut her eyes lightly, as if his words had relieved her. She slipped her hands back under the covers.

I was weeping, and Naoji, his eyes down, sobbed.

Dr. Miyake arrived at this moment and at once administered another injection. Now that Mother had been able to see my uncle, she must have felt that nothing remained for her to live for. She said, "Doctor, please put an end to my suffering soon."

The doctor and my uncle exchanged glances. They did not speak, but tears shone in their eyes.

I went to the dining-room where I prepared some lunch. I took the four plates—for my uncle, the doctor, Naoji, and my aunt—to the Chinese room. I showed Mother the sandwiches my uncle had brought us as a souvenir of Tokyo and put them next to her pillow.

"You are kept so busy," Mother murmured.

We chatted for a while in the Chinese room. My uncle and aunt apparently had business that night in Tokyo which necessitated their return. My uncle handed me an envelope containing some money. He decided that they would return together with Dr. Miyake, who left parting orders with the nurse about the treatment to be followed. It was assumed that Mother would last for another four or five days with the help of the injections. She was still perfectly conscious, and her heart was not too seriously affected.

After I had shown everyone to the gate I went back to Mother's room. She smiled in the particularly intimate way she has always reserved for me. "It must have been a terrible rush for you," she said in a little voice scarcely more than a whisper. Her face was so full of animation, that it seemed almost to shine. She must have been happy to see Uncle, I thought.

Those were the last words that Mother spoke.

About three hours later she passed away . . . in the still autumn twilight, as her pulse was being taken by the nurse, watched over by Naoji and myself, her two children, my beautiful mother, who was the last lady in Japan.

Her face in death was almost unaltered. When my father died his expression had suddenly changed, but Mother's was exactly the same as in life. Only her breathing had stopped. And even that had happened so quietly that we did not know exactly when she had ceased to breathe. The swelling in her face had gone down the previous day, and her cheeks were now smooth as wax. Her pale lips were faintly curved, as though she were smiling. Mother seemed more captivating even than she was in life. The thought that she looked like Mary in a *Pietà* flickered across my mind.

戦闘

CHAPTER SIX

OUTBREAK OF HOSTILITIES

Outbreak of hostilities.

I could not remain forever immersed in my grief. There is something for which I absolutely have to fight. A new ethics. No, even to use the word is hypocrisy. Love. That and nothing else. Just as Rosa Luxemburg had to depend on her new economics for her survival, I cannot go on living unless now I cling with all my force to love. The words of teaching spoken by Jesus to his twelve disciples, when he was about to send them forth to expose the hypocrisies of the scribes and Pharisees and the men of authority of this world and to proclaim to all men without the least hesitation the true love of God, are not entirely inappropriate in my case as well.

Provide neither gold, nor silver, nor brass in your purses,

Nor scrip for your journey, neither two coats, neither shoes, nor yet staves:

Behold, I send you forth as sheep in the midst of wolves; be ye therefore wise as serpents, and harmless as doves.

And fear not them which kill the body, but are not able to kill the soul: but rather fear him which is able to destroy both soul and body in hell.

Think not that I am come to send peace on earth: I came not to send peace, but a sword.

For I am come to set a man at variance against his father, and the daughter against her mother, and the daughter in law against her mother in law.

And a man's foes shall be they of his own household.

He that loveth father or mother more than me is not worthy of me: and he that loveth son or daughter more than me is not worthy of me.

And he that taketh not his cross, and followeth after me, is not worthy of me.

He that findeth his life shall lose it: and he that loseth his life for my sake shall find it.

Outbreak of hostilities.

If because of love I were to swear to obey without fail these teachings of Jesus, to the very letter, I wonder if He would condemn me. Why is physical love bad and spiritual love good? I don't understand. I can't help feeling that they are the same. I would like to boast that I am she who could destroy her body and soul in Gehenna for the sake of a love, for the sake of a passion she could not understand, or for the sake of the sorrow they engendered.

My uncle arranged for the cremation in Izu and the observances in Tokyo. Naoji and I then began our life together, on terms so bad, that even when we met face to face we did not speak. Naoji sold all of Mother's jewelry, styling it "capital" for his publishing venture. When he had exhausted himself in drinking in Tokyo, he would come staggering back, his face deathly pale, like a patient in the last stages of some terrible disease.

One afternoon he turned up with a girl, who looked like a dancer. This made things even more awkward than was usual, and I suggested, "Would it be all right if I went to Tokyo today? I'd like to visit a friend I haven't seen in years. I'll spend two or three nights with her. You won't mind looking after the house, will you? You can have the girl cook for you."

I did not hesitate a moment to take advantage of Naoji's weakness. Thus, quite naturally, displaying the wisdom of the serpent, I stuffed my bag with cosmetics and food and left for Tokyo to see my lover.

Naoji had once told me after a casual inquiry on my part that Mr. Uehara's new house was about twenty minutes' walk from the north exit of the Ogikubo Station on the Tokyo Suburban Line. A blustery autumn wind was blowing that day. It was already growing dark when I got off at Ogikubo Station. I stopped a passerby to ask where Mr. Uehara's house was, but even after being informed I wandered aimlessly for close to an hour through the dark alleys. I felt so forlorn that the tears came. All of a sudden I tripped over a stone in the street, and the strap of my sandals snapped. As I stood there helplessly, wondering what to do, I noticed the name-plate on one of a row of houses to my right, a whitish blob in the dark. I intuitively felt certain that the name Uehara would be written on it. I hobbled over to the entrance, one foot without a sandal. I peered at the plate. Sure enough, it was inscribed "Uehara Jirō," but the interior of the house was dark.

I stood motionless for another moment, at a loss what to do. At length, with a kind of wild desperation, I pressed myself against the door as if about to collapse over it.

"Excuse me," I called, stroking the frame of the window panes with the finger tips of both hands. "Mr. Uehara," I whispered.

There was an answer. But it was a woman's voice.

The entrance door was opened from the inside, and a woman with a thin face, some three or four years older than I and wearing an old-fashioned scent, appeared in the dark hall. There was the flash of a smile as she asked, "Who is it please?" I could detect no malice or threat in her tone.

"Oh, excuse me, I—" But I had missed the chance to say my name. She might have found my love dishonorable. Timidly, almost with servility, I asked, "Is Mr. Uehara at home?"

"No." She looked at my face with an expression of pity, adding, "But he usually goes. . . ."

"Far from here?"

"No." She put one hand to her mouth as if amused. "It's in Ogikubo. If you go to the Shiraishi lunch stand in front of the station, they generally know where he is."

I could have leaped with excitement.

"Oh, what is the matter with your sandal?" She invited me inside. I went into the hall and sat on a bench. Mrs. Uehara gave me a leather strap which I used to replace the broken one. While I busied myself repairing the sandal, she lighted a candle and brought it into the hall. "I'm sorry, but both of our electric bulbs have burned out. It's shocking, isn't it, how terribly dear bulbs have become nowadays and how quickly they burn out? If my husband were at home I could get him to buy another one, but he hasn't come home for two nights running, and my daughter and I have been going to bed early without a penny in our pockets!"

She spoke with a genuinely unself-conscious smile. Behind her stood a thin little girl of about twelve with big eyes and a manner which suggested that she did not often take to people. I did not actually consider them my enemies, but I could be quite sure that one day this woman and child would think of me in those terms and hate me. At this thought I felt as if my love had all of a sudden chilled. I finished changing the strap on my sandal, stood up, and clapped my hands together to brush off the dirt. An unbearably intense foretaste of misery crowded in on me at that moment. I considered rushing into the darkness of the sitting-room to clutch Mrs. Uehara's hand in mine and weep with her. I trembled violently at the thought, only to give it up in sudden dismay when I realized the hypocritical, indescribably unattractive figure I should later make.

"I'm most grateful to you," I said and, making a preposterously polite bow, fled outside. The wind lacerated me. Outbreak of hostilities. I love him, I long for him. I really love him, yes, I really want him. I love him so much I can't help it. I want him so much I can't help it. Yes. I am quite aware that his wife is an unusually sweet person and his little girl is lovely, but I have been stood on God's platform of judgment, and I haven't a trace of guilty conscience. Man was born for love and revolution. There is no reason for God to punish me. I am not in the least wicked. I really love him and there's nothing I won't do to be with him. I'll spend two, three nights sleeping in the fields if necessary. Yes, I will.

I had no trouble finding the Shiraishi lunch stand in front of the station. He was not there.

"He's at Asagaya, I'm sure of it. You head straight for the north exit of the Asagaya Station and, let's see, you go about one hundred fifty yards, I guess. There you'll find a hardware shop, and you go right from there, fifty yards or so, and you'll find a little restaurant called the Willow. Mr. Uehara is having an affair with one of the waitresses, and he spends all his time there. That's where he's taken his business now."

I went to the station, bought a ticket, and boarded a Toyko-bound train. I got off at Asagaya, left by the north exit, and followed directions until I reached the Willow. It was completely deserted.

"He just left in a great crowd of people. They said they were going to spend the night drinking at the Chidori in Nishiogi." The waitress was younger than I, self-possessed, refined, and friendly. I wondered if she was the girl with whom he was having his "affair."

"The Chidori? Where in Nishiogi is that?" I

felt discouraged and on the verge of tears. I wondered suddenly if I had not gone quite insane.

"I don't know exactly, but I think it's somewhere near the station, to the left. In any case I'm sure you can find out if you ask at the police box. But he's not the kind of man to be satisfied with just one place, and he may be trapped somewhere on the way to the Chidori."

"I'll go to the Chidori and see. Good-bye."

Again the train, this time in the opposite direction. I got off at Nishiogi and wandered about in the gale until I found the police box. They told me the way to the Chidori, and I hurried along the dark streets, almost running. I spied the blue lantern of the Chidori and without hesitation slid open the door. In a small smoke-filled room, ten or so people were sitting around a large table, carrying on a rowdy drinking party. Three of them were girls, somewhat younger than I, drinking and smoking like the men.

I stepped inside, cast a glance around the room, and saw him. I felt as if I were dreaming. He was different. Six years. He had become an entirely different person.

Was he my rainbow, M.C., my reason for living? Six years. His hair was as unkempt as before, but it had now become sadly lusterless and thin. His face was bloated and sallow, and the rims of his eyes, a harsh red. Some of his front teeth were missing, and his mouth was continually mumbling. He gave me the feeling of an old monkey squatting with its back hunched over in the corner of a room.

One of the girls noticed me and flashed a signal with her eyes to Mr. Uehara. Still seated, he stuck out his long neck in my direction and expressionlessly motioned me in with his chin. The other members of the party went on with their loud merry-making, seemingly indifferent to me, although they did in fact move a little closer, to make room for me next to Mr. Uehara.

I sat down without saying anything. Mr. Uehara filled my glass with saké to the brim. He then filled his own and muttered hoarsely, "Drink up!"

Our glasses weakly touched and made a sad little clink.

"Guillotine, guillotine, shooshooshoo," shouted someone, and the chant was taken up by another man, "Guillotine, guillotine, shooshooshoo." They banged their glasses together with a loud clanging and gulped down more saké. Group after group took up this meaningless refrain, and again and again they banged their glasses and drained them. It was as if that imbecilic rhythm were furnishing them with the impetus to pour the liquor wildly down their throats.

No sooner did one of their number lurch off,

mumbling his excuses, than a new guest would straggle in and, with a bare nod to Mr. Uehara, wedge his way into the party.

"Mr. Uehara, you know, over there is a place called Ahahah. How would you best pronounce it? Is it Ah-ah-ah or Ahah-ah?" The man leaning forward to ask this question was the actor, Fujita, whom I distinctly remembered having seen on the stage.

"It's Ahah-ah. You should say, Ahah-ah, the liquor at Chidori is not cheap." This from Mr. Uehara.

One of the girls: "The only thing you talk about is money."

A young gentleman: "Is 'two swallows for a farthing' expensive or cheap?"

Another gentleman: "It says in the Bible that you have to pay the last farthing. One man got five talents, another got two talents, and another one—what a horribly long-winded parable that is! Christ's bookkeeping was remarkably detailed."

Another gentleman: "What's more he was a drinker. It's funny how many parables about liquor you find in the Bible. The Bible criticizes people who like wine, but you note it doesn't say a word about the man who *drinks* liquor, only about the man who is fond of it. That proves Christ was quite a drinker. I'll bet he could have put away two quarts at one sitting."

"That's enough, enough. Ye who are frightened by virtue are trying to use Jesus as an excuse.—Let's drink! Guillotine, guillotine, shooshooshoo." Mr. Uehara violently banged his glass against the glass of the youngest and prettiest of the girls and took a deep gulp. The liquor dribbled from the corners of his mouth down to his chin, which he savagely wiped with his palm. Then he gave out with five or six enormous sneezes.

I stood up quietly and went to the next room. I asked the madam, a pale thin woman who looked unwell, for the lavatory. When I crossed through the room on the way back to the party, Chie, the pretty young girl I had noticed before, was standing there, apparently waiting for me.

"Aren't you at all hungry?" she asked with a friendly smile.

"No. I have some bread with me."

"We haven't much to offer, but please take what there is," said the sick-looking madam, leaning wearily over the heater. "Please have a bite in here. If you stay with those drunkards, you won't get a thing to eat all night. Please sit down, here, next to Chie."

"Hey, Kinu, we're out of liquor," shouted a gentleman in the next room.

"Coming!" the maid named Kinu cried as she emerged from the kitchen carrying a tray of ten saké bottles.

"Just a minute," the madam stopped her, "Let's

have two bottles over here." She added with a smile, "And Kinu, I'm sorry to bother you, but please go to Suzuya's and get two bowls of noodles as quick as you can."

I sat next to Chie by the heater and warmed my hands.

"Do sit more comfortably. Here, on a cushion. Hasn't it turned cold! Aren't you drinking anything?" The madam poured some saké from the bottle into her cup and then filled our two cups.

The three of us drank in silence.

"You both can hold your liquor, I see!" the madam said in a curiously intimate tone.

There was a rattle as the front door was opened. "I've brought it, Mr. Uehara," a young man's voice said. "The owner's so tight I barely managed to get ten thousand yen even after holding out for twenty thousand."

"A check?" Mr. Uehara's hoarse voice barked.

"No, it's in cash. I'm sorry."

"That's all right. I'll give you a receipt."

The company continued to roar the drinking song, "Guillotine, guillotine, shooshooshoo" without any let-up even during this conversation.

"How is Naoji?" the madam asked Chie with an earnest expression. I was taken aback.

"How should I know? I'm not his keeper," Chie answered in confusion with a pretty blush.

The madam went on unperturbably, "I wonder if something unpleasant hasn't happened of late between him and Mr. Uehara. They always used to be together."

"I'm told he's taken up dancing. He's probably got a dancer for his sweetheart now."

"Naoji's not a very economical type—women on top of liquor!"

"That's the way Mr. Uehara planned it."

"Naoji's character must be bad. When that kind of spoiled child goes bad—"

"Excuse me," I said, interrupting with a half smile. I thought it would probably be more impolite to keep silent than to speak. "I am Naoji's sister."

The madam, obviously startled, looked again at my face. Chie said in even tones, "You're very much like him. When I saw you standing outside, it gave me quite a turn for a minute. I thought it might be Naoji."

"Oh, indeed?" said the madam, her voice taking on a note of respect, "And for you to come to such a dreadful place! But you knew Mr. Uehara before?"

"Yes, I met him six years ago." I choked over my words and looked down.

The maid entered with the noodles. "Sorry to have kept you waiting."

The madam offered me some. "Please eat before it gets cold."

"Thank you." I thrust my face in the steam rising from the noodles and began to suck them in quickly. I felt as if now I were experiencing what extreme misery is involved in being alive.

Mr. Uehara entered the room, humming faintly, "Guillotine, guillotine, shooshooshoo." He plopped down beside me and without a word handed a large envelope to the madam.

The madam, not so much as glancing inside the envelope, thrust it into a drawer. She said with a laugh, "Don't think you'll get away with just this. I won't be tricked out of the balance."

"I'll bring it. I'll pay the rest next year."

"Am I to believe that?"

Ten thousand yen. How many electric bulbs can you buy with that? I could easily live for a year on that.

There was something wrong about these people. But perhaps, just as it is true of my love, they could not go on living except in the way they do. If it is true that man, once born into the world, must somehow live out his life, perhaps the appearance that people make in order to go through with it, even if it is as ugly as their appearance, should not be despised. To be alive. To be alive. An intolerably immense undertaking before which one can only gasp in apprehension.

"At any rate," said a gentleman's voice in the next

room, "if people like us living in Tokyo cannot henceforth greet one another in the lightest possible way, with the merest suggestion of a hello, life on a civilized plane will be finished. For people nowadays to insist on such virtues as respect or sincerity is like pulling on the feet of a man hanging by the neck. Respect? Sincerity? Rubbish! You can't go on living with them, can you? Unless we can say hello, really casually, there are only three possible courses left—return to the farm, suicide, or becoming a gigolo."

"A poor devil who can't do any one of the three still has a final alternative," said another gentleman. "He can touch Uehara for a loan and get roaring drunk."

Guillotine, guillotine, shooshooshoo. Guillotine, guillotine, shooshooshoo.

"I don't suppose you have anywhere to spend the night, have you?" Mr. Uehara asked half under his breath.

"I?" I was conscious of the snake with its head lifted against itself. Hostility. It was an emotion close to hatred which stiffened my body.

Mr. Uehara, paying no attention to my obvious anger, mumbled on, "Can you sleep in the same room with all the rest of us? It's cold!"

"That's not possible," interpolated the madam. "Have a heart."

Mr. Uehara clicked his tongue against his teeth. "In that case she oughtn't to have come here in the first place."

I remained silent. I could tell at once from something in his tone that he had read my letters and in that instant I knew that he loved me more than anyone else.

He continued, "It can't be helped. Might be a good idea to ask at Fukui's for a bed. Chie, take her over there, won't you? No, on second thought, it would be dangerous in the streets for two women alone. Damned nuisance. I'll have to show her the way myself."

Outside you could tell it was the middle of the night. The wind had died down a little and the sky was filled with shining stars. We walked side by side. I said, "I could perfectly well have slept in the same room with the others."

Mr. Uehara merely grunted sleepily.

"You wanted just the two of us to be together, didn't you?" I spoke with a little laugh.

He twisted his mouth into a bitter smile. "That's the nuisance of it." I was intensely, almost painfully, aware of the fact that it was love he felt for me.

"You drink a great deal. Is it like that every night?"

"Every day. From morning."

"Does the liquor taste so good?"

"It stinks."

Something in his voice made me shudder. "How is your work coming?"

"No good. Whatever I write now is stupid and depressing. The twilight of life. The twilight of art. The twilight of mankind. What bathos!"

"Utrillo," I murmured before I knew it.

"Yes, Utrillo. They say he's still alive. A victim of alcohol. A corpse. His paintings of the last ten years have been incredibly vulgar and worthless without exception."

"It's not only just Utrillo, is it? All the other masters too."

"Yes, they've all lost their vitality. But the new shoots have also lost their vitality, blasted in the bud. Frost. It's as though an unseasonable frost had fallen all over the whole world."

His arm lay lightly around my shoulders. It was as if my body were being enveloped in his cape, but I did not deny him. I nestled all the closer as we walked slowly on.

The branches of trees beside the road. Branches destitute of even a single leaf, narrow, sharp, stabbing the night sky. "Branches are beautiful, aren't they?" I whispered, almost to myself.

"You mean the harmony between the blossoms and the black branches?" he asked in a somewhat confused tone.

"No, I'm not referring to the blossoms or the leaves or the buds or anything else. I love branches. Even when they're perfectly bare, they're fully alive. They're not a bit like dead branches."

"You mean only Nature retains her vitality?" He thereupon gave several more of his tremendous sneezes.

"Have you caught a cold?"

"No, I haven't. I have a funny habit—whenever my drunkenness reaches the saturation point, all at once I start to sneeze like that. It's something of a barometer of my intoxication."

"What about love?"

"What?"

"Is there someone? Someone who is approaching the saturation point?"

"Don't make fun of me! Women are all alike—they're so damned complicated. Guillotine, guillotine, shooshooshoo. As a matter of fact there *is* someone, no, half a someone."

"Did you read my letters?"

"Yes."

"What answer have you to make?"

"I don't like the aristocracy. There's always a kind of offensive arrogance hovering around them. Your brother Naoji is a great success for an aristocrat, but every now and then even he displays an affectation I simply can't put up with. I am a farmer's boy, and I never go by a stream like this one without an almost painfully sharp recollection of the days when I used to fish for silver carp or scoop up minnows with a net in the streams at home."

We were walking on a road which followed a stream that flowed with a faint rustle at the bottom of the darkness.

"You aristocrats are not only absolutely incapable of understanding our feelings, but you despise them."

"What about Turgenev?"

"He was an aristocrat. That's why I dislike him."

"Even his *Sportsman's Sketches?*"

"That book—it's his only one—is not bad."

"It really captures the feeling of village life."

"He was a rustic aristocrat—shall we compromise on that?"

"I'm also a country girl now. I cultivate a field. A poor country girl."

"Do you still love me?" His voice was rough. "Do you want a child from me?"

I did not answer.

His face approached mine with the force of a landslide, and I was furiously kissed. The kisses reeked of desire. I wept as I accepted them. My tears were bitter, like tears of shame over a humiliation. The tears poured from my eyes.

As we walked again, side by side, he spoke. "I've made a mess of it—I've fallen for you." He laughed.

I was incapable of laughter. I contracted my brows and pursed my lips. If I were to have expressed my feelings in words, it would have been something like "It can't be helped." I realized that I was dragging my feet in a desolate walk.

"I've made a mess of it," the man said again. "Shall we go through with it?"

"Don't strike a pose!"

"You devil!" Mr. Uehara rapped my shoulder with his fist and again gave a great sneeze.

Everyone seemed to be asleep at Mr. Fukui's house.

"Telegram, telegram! Mr. Fukui, it's a telegram!" Mr. Uehara shouted, beating on the door.

"Is that you, Uehara?" a man's voice called.

"Quite correct. The prince and the princess have come to beg a night's lodgings. It's so cold that all I can do is sneeze, and after going to so much trouble, our lovers' journey is winding up as a comedy."

The front door was opened. A short bald man of about fifty in gaudy pajamas greeted us with a curiously shy smile.

"Please." This was the only word Mr. Uehara spoke as he charged into the house, without so much as removing his coat. "Your atelier is hopelessly cold.

I'll take the second-floor room. Come on." He took me by the hand and led me through the hall to a staircase at the end, which we climbed. We entered a dark room. Mr. Uehara switched on the lights.

"It's like a private dining-room in a restaurant, isn't it?" I said.

"The tastes of the *nouveau riche*. Still, it's much too good for a rotten artist like Fukui. When you've got the devil's own luck, you're immune from the usual run of disasters. Such people must be utilized. Well, to bed, to bed."

He started pulling bedding out of the cupboard as if he were in his own home. "You sleep here. I'm going. I'll come for you tomorrow morning. The toilet is downstairs and to the right." He thumped so loudly down the stairs that it sounded as though he had rolled down. That was all. The place became absolutely still.

I switched off the light again, removed my velvet coat made of material Father once had brought back as a souvenir from abroad, and crawled into bed still in my kimono, barely loosening my obi. My body felt heavy, probably because of the liquor I had drunk when I was already fatigued, and I soon dozed off.

I don't know when it happened, but I opened my eyes to find him lying next to me. For almost an hour I maintained a determined wordless resistance.

Suddenly I felt sorry for him and yielded.

"Is this life you are leading the only relief you can get?"

"That's about it."

"But doesn't it tell on your body? I'm sure you've coughed blood."

"How do you know? As a matter of fact, I had a rather serious bout the other day, but I haven't told anyone."

"It's the same smell as before Mother died."

"I drink out of desperation. Life is too dreary to endure. The misery, loneliness, crampedness—they're heartbreaking. Whenever you can hear the gloomy sighs of woe from the four walls around you, you know that there's not a chance of happiness existing just for you. What feelings do you suppose a man has when he realizes that he will never know happiness or glory as long as he lives? Hard work. All that amounts to is food for the wild beasts of hunger. There are too many pitiful people.—Is that a pose again?"

"No."

"Only love. Just as you wrote in your letters."

"Yes."

My love was extinguished.

When the room became faintly light, I stared at the face of the man sleeping beside me. It was the face of a man soon to die. It was an exhausted face.

The face of a victim. A precious victim.

My man. My rainbow. My Child. Hateful man. Unprincipled man.

It seemed to me then a face of a beauty unmatched in the whole world. My breast throbbed with the sensation of resuscitated love. I kissed him as I stroked his hair.

The sad, sad accomplishment of love.

Mr. Uehara, his eyes still shut, took me in his arms. "I was all wrong. What do you expect of a farmer's son?"

I could never leave him.

"I am happy now. Even if I were to hear the four walls all shriek in anguish, my feeling of happiness would still be at the saturation point. I am so happy I could sneeze."

Mr. Uehara laughed. "But it's too late now. It's dusk already."

"It's morning!"

That morning my brother Naoji committed suicide.

遺

書

CHAPTER SEVEN / THE TESTAMENT

Naoji's testament:

Kazuko.

It's no use. I'm going.

I cannot think of the slightest reason why I should have to go on living.

Only those who wish to go on living should.

Just as a man has the right to live, he ought also to have the right to die.

There is nothing new in what I am thinking: it is simply that people have the most inexplicable aversion to this obvious—not to say primitive—idea and refuse to come out with it plainly.

Those who wish to go on living can always man-

age to survive whatever obstacles there may be. That is splendid of them, and I daresay that what people call the glory of mankind is comprised of just such a thing. But I am convinced that dying is not a sin.

It is painful for the plant which is myself to live in the atmosphere and light of this world. Somewhere an element is lacking which would permit me to continue. I am wanting. It has been all I could do to stay alive up to now.

When I entered high school and first came in contact with friends of an aggressively sturdy stock, boys who had grown up in a class entirely different from my own, their energy put me on the defensive, and in the effort not to give in to them, I had recourse to drugs. Half in a frenzy I resisted them. Later, when I became a soldier, it was as a last resort for staying alive that I took to opium. You can't understand what I was going through, can you?

I wanted to become coarse, to be strong—no, brutal. I thought that was the only way I could qualify myself as a "friend of the people." Liquor was not enough. I was perpetually prey to a terrible dizziness. That was why I had no choice but to take to drugs. I had to forget my family. I had to oppose my father's blood. I had to reject my mother's gentleness. I had to be cold to my sister. I thought that otherwise I would not be able to secure an admission ticket for the rooms of the people.

I became coarse. I learned to use coarse language. But it was half—no, sixty per cent—a wretched imposture, an odd form of petty trickery. As far as the "people" were concerned, I was a stuck-up prig who put them all on edge with my affected airs. They would never really unbend and relax with me. On the other hand, it is now impossible for me to return to those salons I gave up. Even supposing that my coarseness is sixty per cent artifice, the remaining forty per cent is genuine now. The intolerable gentility of the upper-class salon turns my stomach, and I could not endure it for an instant. And those distinguished gentlemen, those eminent citizens, as they are called, would be revolted by my atrocious manners and soon ostracize me. I can't return to the world I abandoned, and all the "people" give me (with a fulsome politeness that is filled with malice) is a seat in the visitor's gallery.

It may be true that in any society defective types with low vitality like myself are doomed to perish, not because of what they think or anything else, but because of themselves. I have, however, some slight excuse to offer. I feel the overwhelming pressure of circumstances which make it extremely difficult for me to live.

All men are alike.

I wonder if that might be a philosophy. I don't believe that the person who first thought up this extraordinary expression was a religious man or a philosopher or an artist. The expression assuredly oozed forth from some public bar like a grub, without anyone's having pronounced it, an expression fated to overturn the whole world and render it repulsive.

This astonishing assertion has absolutely no connection with democracy, or with Marxism for that matter. Without question it was the remark at a bar hurled by an ugly man at a handsome one. It was simple irritation, or, if you will, jealousy and had nothing to do with ideology or anything of the kind.

But what began as an angry cry of jealousy in a public bar assumed a peculiarly doctrinaire cast of countenance to strut among the common people, and a remark which obviously had no possible connection with democracy or Marxism attached itself before one knew it onto political and economic doctrine and created an unbelievably sordid mess.

I imagine that Mephisto himself would have found the trick of converting such an absurd utterance into doctrine so great an affront to his conscience that he would have hesitated over it.

All men are alike.

What a servile remark that is. An utterance that degrades itself at the same time that it degrades men, lacking in all pride, seeking to bring about the abandonment of all effort. Marxism proclaims the superi-

ority of the workers. It does not say that they are all the same. Democracy proclaims the dignity of the individual. It does not say that they are all the same. Only the lout will assert, "Yes, no matter how much he puts on, he's just a human being, same as the rest of us."

Why does he say "same." Can't he say "superior"? The vengeance of the slave mentality!

The statement is obscene and loathsome. I believe that all of the so-called "anxiety of the age"—men frightened by one another, every known principle violated, effort mocked, happiness denied, beauty defiled, honor dragged down—originates in this one incredible expression.

I must admit, although I was entirely convinced of the hideousness of the expression, that it intimidated me. I trembled with fear, felt shy and embarrassed, whatever I attempted to do, throbbed ceaselessly with anxiety, and was powerless to act. I needed more than ever the momentary peace that the vertigo of drink and drugs could afford. Then everything went astray.

I must be weak. There must be a serious deficiency somewhere. I can just hear the old lout saying with a snicker, "What's all this rationalizing for? Anyone can see that he's a playboy from way back, a lazy, lecherous, selfish child of pleasure." Up to now when people have spoken of me that way I have always nodded vaguely in embarrassment, but now that I am on the point of death, I would like to say a word by way of protest.

Kazuko.

Please believe me.

I have never derived the least joy out of amusements. Perhaps that is a sign of the impotence of pleasure. I ran riot and threw myself into wild diversions out of the simple desire to escape from my own shadow—being an aristocrat.

I wonder if we are to blame, after all. Is it our fault that we were born aristocrats? Merely because we were born in such a family, we are condemned to spend our whole lives in humiliation, apologies, and abasement, like so many Jews.

I should have died sooner. But there was one thing: Mama's love. When I thought of that I couldn't die. It's true, as I have said, that just as man has the right to live as he chooses, he has the right to die when he pleases, and yet as long as my mother remained alive, I felt that the right to death would have to be left in abeyance, for to exercise it would have meant killing her too.

Now even if I die, no one will be so grieved as to do himself bodily harm. No, Kazuko, I know just how much sadness my death will cause you. Undoubtedly you will weep when you learn the news—apart, of course, from such ornamental sentimentality as you may indulge in—but if you will please try to think of my joy at being liberated completely from the suffering of living and this hateful life itself, I believe that your sorrow will gradually dissolve.

Any man who criticizes my suicide and passes judgment on me with an expression of superiority, declaring (without offering the least help) that I should have gone on living my full complement of days, is assuredly a prodigy among men quite capable of tranquilly urging the Emperor to open a fruit shop.

Kazuko.

I am better off dead. I haven't the capacity to stay alive. I haven't the strength to quarrel with people over money. I can't even touch people for a hand-out. Even when I went drinking with Mr. Uehara, I always paid my share of the bill. He hated me for it and called it the cheap pride of the aristocracy, but it was not out of pride that I paid. I was too frightened to be able to drink or to hold a woman in my arms with money that had come from his work. I used to pass it off by saying that I acted out of respect for Mr. Uehara's writings, but that was a lie. I don't really understand myself why I did it. It was just that being paid for by other people was somehow disturbing. It was in particular intolerably painful and repugnant to be entertained with money gained by another person's own efforts.

And when I was reduced to taking money and belongings from my own house, causing Mama and you to suffer, it didn't bring me the slightest pleasure. The publishing business I planned was just a front to conceal my embarrassment—I was not at all in earnest. For all of my stupidity I was at least aware that someone who could not even stand being bought a drink would be utterly incapable of making money, and there was no use in being earnest.

Kazuko.

We have become impoverished. While I was alive and still had the means, I always thought of paying for others, but now we can only survive by being paid for by others.

Kazuko.

Why must I go on living after what has happened? It's useless. I am going to die. I have a poison that kills without pain. I got it when I was a soldier and have kept it ever since.

Kazuko, you are beautiful (I have always been proud of my beautiful mother and sister) and you are intelligent. I haven't any worries about you. I lack even the qualifications to worry. I can only blush —like a robber who sympathizes with his victim! I feel sure that you will marry, have children, and manage to survive through your husband.

Kazuko.

I have a secret.

I have concealed it for a long, long time. Even when I was on the battlefield, I brooded over it and dreamed of her. I can't tell you how many times I awoke only to find I had wept in my sleep.

I shall never be able to reveal her name to anyone, but I thought that I would at least tell you, my sister, everything about her, since I am now on the point of death. I discover, however, that I am still so terribly afraid that I dare not speak her name.

And yet I feel that if I die keeping the secret absolute and leave the world with it locked within my breast undisclosed, when my body is cremated the insides of my breast will remain dank-smelling and unburned. This thought so disquiets me that I must tell you, and only you, about it—indirectly, imprecisely, as if I were relating some odd bit of fiction. And even if I call it fiction you will, I am sure, recognize immediately of whom I write. It is less fiction than a kind of thin disguise achieved by the use of false names.

Do you know, I wonder?

I imagine that you do know about her, although you probably have never met. She is a little older than you. Her eyes are the true Japanese shape, like an almond, and she always wears her hair (which has never been subjected to a permanent) in a very conservative Japanese style, tightly pulled back from her face. Her clothes are shabby but spotless and worn with a real distinction. She is the wife of a certain middle-aged painter who won sudden fame after the war by producing a rapid succession of paintings in a new idiom. The painter is very wild and dissipated, but his wife always goes about with a gentle smile on her face, pretending to be undisturbed by his behavior.

I stood up. "I must be going now."

She also rose and walked, with no suggestion of reserve, to my side. "Why?" she asked, looking at my face. Her voice had quite its ordinary timbre. She held her head a little to the side, as if really in doubt, and looked me straight in the eyes. In her eyes there was neither malice nor pretence. Normally, if my eyes had met hers, I would have averted them in confusion, but that one time I felt not the least particle of shyness. For sixty seconds or more, our faces about a foot apart, I stared into her eyes, feeling terribly happy. I finally said with a smile, "But—"

"He'll be back soon," she said, her face grave.

It suddenly occurred to me that what people call "honesty" might well refer to just such an expression. I wondered if what the word originally meant was not something lovable like that expression, rather than the stern virtue smelling of textbooks of morality.

"I'll come again."

"Do."

Our whole conversation from beginning to end was completely unimportant. One summer afternoon I had called at the painter's apartment. He was out, but expected back at any moment. His wife suggested that I wait, and for half an hour I had read magazines. When there were still no signs of his returning, I got up to take my leave. That was all there was to it, but I fell painfully in love with her eyes as they were that day.

You might even describe them as "noble." I can only say with certainty that none of the aristocrats among whom we lived—leaving Mama aside—was capable of that unguarded expression of "honesty."

Then it happened one winter evening that I was struck by her profile. I had been drinking since morning with the painter in his apartment, and we had roared with laughter as we abused the so-called "Japanese men of culture." The artist fell asleep and soon was loudly snoring. I was also dozing off when a blanket was gently thrown over me. I opened my eyes a crack and saw her sitting quietly with her daughter in her arms next to the apartment window, against the clear blue sky of a Tokyo winter's evening. Her regular profile, its outlines clear-cut with the brilliance of a Renaissance portrait, floated against the background of the pale blue of the distant sky. There was nothing of coquetry or desire in the kindness which had impelled her to throw the blanket over me. Might not the word "humanity" be revived to use of such a moment? She had acted almost without consciousness of what she did, as a natural gesture of sympathy for another person, and now she was staring at the distant sky, in an atmosphere of stillness exactly like a painting.

I shut my eyes. I felt sweep over me a wave of love and longing. Tears forced their way through my eyelids, and I pulled the blanket over my head.

Kazuko.

At first I used to visit the painter's house because I was intoxicated by the unique idiom of his works and the fanatical passion hidden in them, but as I grew more intimate, his lack of culture, his irresponsibility, and his dirtiness disillusioned me. I was drawn in inverse proportion to the beauty of feeling of his wife. No, it was rather that I was in love with someone of true affections. I came to visit the painter's house solely in the hope of getting a glimpse of his wife.

I am convinced that if anything at all of artistic nobility is discoverable in the painter's works, it is most probably a reflection of his wife's gentle spirit.

The painter—I will now come out with exactly what I feel—is nothing but a clever businessman with a great capacity for drink and debauchery. When he needs money for his pleasures, he daubs something together which he sells at a high price by posing as a great artist and by taking advantage of the current fads. His only assets are the shamelessness of the country boor, a stupid confidence, and a sharp talent for business.

He probably has no comprehension whatsoever of the paintings of other artists, foreign or Japanese, and I doubt whether he even understands what his own pictures are all about. What it amounts to is that when driven by financial pressure he frantically splashes paint onto a canvas.

Incredibly enough, he apparently has no doubts, shame, or fears about the rubbish he produces. In fact, he is quite puffed up about it. And, given that he is the kind of man who does not understand what he himself has painted, one cannot expect him to appreciate other people's work. Far from it—all he does is carp and rail.

In other words, although he is fond of ranting on about the agonies he suffers in his life of decadence, in point of fact he is just a stupid country bumpkin who realized his dreams by coming to the big city and scoring a success on a scale quite unimagined even to himself. This so inflated his ego that now he spends his time in one round of pleasure after another.

Once I said to him, "It makes me feel so embarrassed and afraid if, when all my friends are out amusing themselves, I study by myself, that I can't do a thing. That's why, even when I don't feel the least like going out, I join the crowd."

The middle-aged artist answered, "What! That's what they mean, I suppose, by an aristocratic disposition. It turns my stomach. When I see some people having a good time, I think what I'm missing if I don't do the same, and I really throw myself into it."

His answer was so pat that it made me despise him from the heart. No suffering lies behind his dissipation. On the contrary, he takes pride in his stupid pleasures. A genuine idiot-hedonist.

I could relate any number of other unpleasant things about this artist, but after all he doesn't concern you. Besides, now that I am about to die, I remember also the long acquaintanceship we have had, and I feel so nostalgic for him that my impulse is to go out drinking with him once more. I don't bear him any hatred. He has many endearing qualities, and I shall say no more of him.

I only would like you to know how excruciating it was for me to spend my time in fruitless yearning for his wife. That is all. But now that you know, there is absolutely no necessity for you to play the busybody by informing anyone of this in the hopes of "winning recognition" of the love your brother bore when he was alive, or any such thing. It is quite sufficient if just you know it and are kind enough to murmur to yourself, "Was that what happened?" And, to voice one more hope, I should be very happy if this shameful confession of mine made at least you, if no one else, understand better the sufferings I have gone through.

Once I dreamed I held hands with his wife, and I knew at once that she had loved me from long before. Even after I waked from my dreams, the warmth of her fingers remained in the palm of my hand. I told myself that I would have to resign myself to that much and nothing more. It was not that I was intimidated by the morality of the thing, but that half-mad, no, virtual maniac of an artist terrified me. As part of my resolve to give her up, I attempted to direct the flames in my breast toward another object and recklessly threw myself into wild orgies with all sorts of women, whichever one happened to be available, so outrageously in fact that even the artist looked disapprovingly at me one night. I wanted somehow to free myself from his wife's enchantment, to forget it, to have everything over and done with. But it was no use. I am, it would seem, a man who can only love one woman. I can state it quite positively—I have never once felt any of my women friends was beautiful or lovable except her.

Kazuko.

I would like once before I die to write her name.

Suga.

That is her name.

Yesterday I brought a dancer here (a woman of ingrained stupidity) for whom I have not the least affection. I never dreamed when I arrived that I would be dying this morning, although I had as a matter of fact had a premonition that it would certainly not be long before I was dead. The reason why I brought the girl here this morning was that she had begged me to take her on a trip somewhere, and I was so exhausted by my dissipation in Tokyo that I thought it might not be a bad idea to rest here for a couple of days with that stupid woman. I knew it would be rather awkward for you, but the two of us came anyway. When you left for your friend's place in Tokyo, the thought flashed into my head "If I am going to kill myself, now is the time."

I always used to think that I would like to die in my room in the house in Nishikata Street. Somehow I was repelled by the thought of dying in some public place and having my corpse handled by the rabble. But the house in Nishikata Street passed into other people's hands, and I realized that now I had no choice but to die in this house in the country. Even so, when I told myself that you would be the one to find my body and imagined how alarmed this would make you, I felt so hesitant about killing myself that I could not possibly have gone through with it.

And now this chance. You are not here, and in-

stead an extremely dull-witted dancer will be the one to discover my suicide.

Last night we drank together and I put her to bed in the foreign-style room on the second floor. I laid out bedding for myself in the room downstairs where Mama died. Then I began to write this wretched memoir.

Kazuko.

I have no room for hope. Good-bye.

In the last analysis my death is a natural one—man cannot live exclusively for principles. I have one request to make of you, which embarrasses me very much. You remember the hemp kimono of Mother's which you altered so that I could wear it next summer? Please put it in my coffin. I wanted to wear it.

The night has dawned. I have made you suffer a long time.

Good-bye.

My drunkenness from last night has entirely worn off. I shall die sober.

Once more, good-bye.

Kazuko.

I am, after all, an aristocrat.

CHAPTER EIGHT / VICTIMS

Nightmares.

Everyone is leaving me.

I took care of everything after Naoji's death. For a month I lived alone in the house in the country.

Then I wrote Mr. Uehara what was probably to be my last letter, with a feeling of futility.

It seems that you too have abandoned me. No, it seems rather as though you are gradually forgetting me.

But I am happy. I have become pregnant, as I had hoped. I feel as if I had now lost everything. Nevertheless, the little being within me has become the source of my solitary smiles.

I cannot possibly think of it in terms of a "hideous mistake" or anything of the sort. Recently I have come to understand why such things as war, peace, unions, trade, politics exist in the world. I don't suppose you know. That's why you will always be unhappy. I'll tell you why—it is so that women will give birth to healthy babies.

From the first I never set much stock by your character or your sense of responsibility. The only thing in my mind was to succeed in the adventure of my wholehearted love. Now that my desire has been fulfilled, there is in my heart the stillness of a marsh in a forest.

I think I have won.

Even if Mary gives birth to a child who is not her husband's, if she has a shining pride, they become a holy mother and child.

I disregarded the old morality with a clear conscience, and I will have as a result the satisfaction of a good baby.

I presume that since last we met you have been continuing your life of decadence or whatever it is called, drinking with the ladies and gentlemen to the tune of "Guillotine, guillotine." I have no intention of suggesting that you give that life up. It will, after all, most likely be the form your last struggle takes.

I no longer have the desire to say, "Give up your drinking, take care of your health, lead a long life, carry through your splendid career," or any of the other hypocritical injunctions. For all I know, you may earn the gratitude of later people more by recklessly pursuing your life of vice than by your "splendid career."

Victims. Victims of a transitional period of morality. That is what we both certainly are.

The revolution must be taking place somewhere, but the old morality persists unchanged in the world around us and lies athwart our way. However much the waves on the surface of the sea may rage, the water at the bottom, far from experiencing a revolution, lies motionless, awake but feigning sleep.

But I think that in this first engagement, I have been able to push back the old morality, however little. And I intend to fight a second and a third engagement together with the child who will be born.

To give birth to the child of the man I love, and to raise him, will be the accomplishment of my moral revolution.

Even if you forget me, and even if on account of

drink you destroy your life, I believe I shall be able to go on living healthily, for the sake of the accomplishment of my revolution.

Not long ago I learned from a certain person in considerable detail about the worthlessness of your character. All the same, it is you who have given me this strength, you who have put the rainbow of revolution in my breast. It is you who have given an object to my life.

I am proud of you and I trust I shall make the child who is to be born feel proud of you.

A bastard and its mother.

We will live in perpetual struggle with the old morality, like the sun.

You, too, please try to continue to fight your struggle.

The revolution is far from taking place. It needs more, many more valuable, unfortunate victims.

In the present world, the most beautiful thing is a victim.

There was another little victim.

Mr. Uehara.

I do not feel like asking anything more of you, but on behalf of that little victim I should like to ask your indulgence in one thing.

I should like your wife to take my child in her arms—even once will do—and let me say then, "Naoji secretly had this child from a certain woman."

Why do this? That is one thing which I cannot tell anyone. No, I am not even sure myself why I want it done. But I am most anxious that you do this for me. Please do it for the sake of Naoji, that little victim.

Are you irritated? Even if you are, please bear with me. Think this the one offense of a deserted woman who is being forgotten, and please, I beg you, grant it.

To M.C. My Comedian.